HIDDEN WORLD

STANTON A. COBLENTZ

AIRMONT

AIRMONT PUBLISHING COMPANY, INC.
22 EAST 60TH STREET · NEW YORK 22

HIDDEN WORLD

An AIRMONT BOOK published by arrangement with
Thomas Bouregy and Company, Inc.

PRINTING HISTORY
Bouregy edition published August, 1957
Airmont edition published June, 1964

PUBLISHED SIMULTANEOUSLY IN THE DOMINION OF CANADA
BY THE RYERSON PRESS, TORONTO

PRINTED IN THE UNITED STATES OF AMERICA
BY THE COLONIAL PRESS, INC., CLINTON, MASSACHUSETTS

CONTENTS

1. CAVE-IN

It is now six years since Clay and I were given up by the world as lost. One fact in the case, and one only, may be remembered by the public. In the autumn of 1951, newspapers throughout the country reported that Philip Clay and Frank Comstock, mining engineers, had disappeared in the depths of a silver mine in Nevada.

I shall not linger over the preliminaries, except to state that Philip Clay and I had been partners ever since our graduation from Western Institute of Mining in 1939. We had spent all our time in experiments and enterprises in the back regions of Montana, Idaho, and other states of the mountain belt. In September, 1951, we were called to pass judgment on the old Carlson Flat Silver Mine, which an Eastern syndicate was just reopening. The mine was located in a particularly inaccessible section of central Nevada, Carlson Flat— as desolate a spot as you could imagine. We were at the edge of a narrow barren plateau, just beneath a stony ridge that beetled a thousand feet above. No matter; we spent most of the time in that long-abandoned mine, whose shafts were not only unusually dank and narrow, but exceptionally deep.

It was on the third day that we decided to inspect the farthest and deepest section of the diggings. Accompanied by two or three workmen, and an official of the company, we made our way tortuously through galleries that seemed miles long, and accomplished the dim descent hundreds of feet beneath the desert floor. Every now and then, as we groped and fumbled silently downward, I seemed to feel a sudden faint trembling of the earth.

"Feel that?" I demanded of Clay, after one tremor.

But he merely snapped, "Feel what?"

"Seemed like an earthquake to me!" I muttered.

"Earthquake? How the devil could it be? We're out of the earthquake belt, aren't we?"

I mumbled in the affirmative, but was not reassured.

A few minutes later, we had reached the mine's lowest limits. I pushed on with Clay, ahead of our companions, and was just turning my flashlight on an ore-producing ledge at the bottom of the gallery when . . . it happened.

Like many of life's crises, it was all over in a minute. The earth gave a convulsive lurch, like a ship's deck during a storm at sea. I heard Clay's sharp exclamation, and the startled shout of our companions, down the tunnel. I heard the crunching, grinding, and groaning of the earth, and a low rumbling from far subterranean depths; then I was pitched headlong to the floor as the ground heaved beneath us. I could see a gleam of panic in Clay's eyes as he tried to clutch a projecting spike of rock; then, as the commotion momentarily subsided, I almost regained my feet—only to be hurled down again.

As I tried to get up, my ears rang with the thunder of falling rock. The roof of the gallery had collapsed; by the wavering rays of a flashlight, we saw ourselves entombed. But even as this realization swept across our minds, there was a fresh roaring in our ears. A huge rock crashed down from the roof, and then, at our feet, the earth groaned and opened, and a broad black fissure spread out beneath us.

Desperately, like mountain climbers on a crumbling precipice, we tried to hold our balance on the narrow floor of our prison. We could see the fissure widening, spreading out; then the light in Clay's flashlight flickered and died. . . .

In the darkness, clutching instinctively at the overhanging rocks, we felt ourselves slipping. I heard Clay's cry; I heard the uproar of sliding earth and rock; I felt my arms and shoulders bruised. There was a sense of suffocation, of being buried beneath tons of dead matter; then . . . quietness.

I have always marveled that Clay and I lived through the cataclysm. Probably we owe our survival to the fact that the fissure, far from being perpendicular, sloped at an angle of thirty or forty degrees, so that, while rolling over and over in our descent, we were spared a direct drop.

It may have been minutes, or it may have been hours later; but when I came to myself, it was with a dull aching in the head, and a sensation of soreness in every limb and muscle.

"Where are we?" I gasped.

"Where are we? I wish I knew," came in mumbled accents from an unseen figure.

"Much hurt, Phil?" I jerked out, striving to locate Clay amid the blackness as I started to extricate myself from the stones and dust.

"No, not hurt much!" came Clay's drawled reply. "A few little cuts and bruises, more or less, and one black eye. But I couldn't use the eye down here, anyway! How about you, Frank?"

"I'm all right," I said, as cheerfully as I could, considering that I felt as if I had been through a threshing machine.

"We'll sure be able to collect big damages! Don't know where we are, Frank, but I wouldn't mind being anywhere else. Where are you?"

It took us several minutes to find each other. At length, guided by the sound of our voices, we brushed shoulders in the darkness. Thereafter, we clasped hands to keep together.

After a few minutes, we passed the debris-littered area, and found a smooth stone floor slanting beneath our feet. And, a yard or two to each side of us, our groping fingers discovered a polished stone wall.

Clay whistled. "Who'd have thought the mine reached this far down?"

"Mine?" I returned derisively. "When did you ever see a mine with polished walls?"

"Well, what is it if not a mine? Just tell me that!"

Not being able to answer, I remained silent, as we continued on down those uncanny corridors.

For another ten or fifteen minutes we plodded on without a word. The walls were still as polished and regular as ever, the blackness as absolute and unbroken; now we felt an occasional jarring of the earth at uneven intervals. It grew a little more pronounced, but was less disturbing as we became used to it.

Then, unexpectedly, the gallery curved, turning almost at right angles. And as we felt our way around the bend, the tunnel curved again even more sharply; then curved once more; while, adding to our bewilderment, we discovered several side-galleries branching off in various directions.

At the same time, the thuddings of the earth grew more pronounced, accompanied by rumblings and reverberations of terrifying force and insistency. Crash after crash burst upon us, as if from some remote storm center.

What could it be? Some volcanic disturbance in the depths of the earth? So we were inclined to believe as, sweating with fear, we halted for a consultation. In another moment, might we not feel the reek of sulphur in our nostrils?

Groping around another turn in the gallery, we were startled to see an indistinct patch of light far ahead. Vaguely rectangular in shape, and of an unearthly greenish hue, it wavered and flickered strangely, at times almost disappearing, at times flaring to a hectic, momentary brilliance, shot through with flashes of red, orange, and violet. Simultaneously, the far-off thunders grew more deep-throated.

"Lord," muttered Clay, "you could almost believe the old yarns about Old Nick and his court of devils!"

"Court of devils?" I tossed back. "The only devils are in your imagination, Phil! It's clear enough what's wrong. The earth is going through a little fit of indigestion. Most likely it'll clear up any moment."

These words were barely out of my mouth when the earth gave a lurch that knocked us both off our feet. And for an instant the light from down the gallery became a sunlike glare, by which I caught a glimpse of Clay's harried face, one eye half closed and a long gash across his forehead.

Probably I did not present a more inviting sight, for, as we both picked ourselves up, he exclaimed, "Say, old fellow, I ought to have your picture now!"

I didn't bother to reply, but started away again along the gallery, whose walls were now and then dimly visible by the flickering light ahead. To our astonishment, we saw that the ceiling formed a perfect triangle, an inverted V like the roof of a house. Here was the handiwork of man—yet what man before us had penetrated these labyrinths?

But it was useless to speculate. We had to go forward and find out. As we approached the light, we were relieved to find that the earth trembled less violently and less often, and that the illumination down the passageway grew more steady and distinct.

"See, Phil, I told you the earthquakes would be over soon!" I told my companion. But Clay didn't reply; he merely quickened his footsteps.

At last we were drawing near the mysterious light. It had now ceased to flicker, and shone with a steady greenish-yellow glare, so bright as to fill the gallery with a weird radiance, wherein we could clearly distinguish each other's features. The source of the light, however, remained an enigma.

In a few minutes we had reached the corridor's end, and, turning sharply, found ourselves in a wider passageway penetrated by scores of cross-galleries and terminating, about a hundred yards beyond, in a perfect blaze of greenish light.

"Lord in heaven!" exclaimed Clay, as we reached the new thoroughfare. "Are we dreaming? Or am I simply crazy?"

"Guess we're both crazy!" I muttered. "Come on, let's find out what's what!"

"Might as well die exploring!" he conceded.

I now noticed for the first time that Clay was walking with a slight limp; I also noticed that his rude mining garb was not only soiled with streaks and blotches of black, but was ripped and torn in a hundred places. But my own clothes were in an equally sorry condition.

As we slowly covered the hundred yards to the end of the second gallery, I could see the bleak furrows on Clay's long, lean, battered face. He stroked his disheveled red hair. "Say, Frank, if anything happens to me, see that my mother gets my watch as a remembrance. Tell her I was thinking of her at the last—"

"Tell her yourself!" I interrupted. "Haven't you as good a chance as I of getting out of this infernal mess?"

"Suppose I have, at that! Guess it's both of us, or neither!"

Our conversation was interrupted by our arrival at the end of the second gallery. Clay, preceding me by half a dozen feet, stopped short and gasped. I heard his swift exclamation, and gained his side; then I, too, seemed to have lost my tongue.

How can I describe the scene which had suddenly unfolded before us? Surely, the discoverer of a new planet could not have had a deeper sense of awe! For here was, literally, a new world. The gallery had ended as if on the brink of a precipice; we were staring down, through yellowish-green abysses, into a chasm as wide and deep as the Grand Canyon of Arizona. As wide and deep, but by no means as irregular, by no means as narrow at the bottom. Unlike the great gorge of the Colorado, this showed no unevenness of structure; sheer stone walls, straight and precipitous as the walls of a room, shot down beneath us a mile deep. Sheer stone walls, equally precipitous and straight, rose opposite us at a distance of more than a mile, and between them spread the bare, level floor of the cavern, which reached to our right and left to an incalculable remoteness.

There was such an atmosphere of unreality about it all that only by degrees could I absorb the details. There was the gentle curve of the ceiling, which, arching but a few hundred feet above us, revealed fantastic figures, vaguely man-shaped, standing out sharply in cameo. There was a multitude of greenish-yellow bulbs which, square or rounded or elongated into rods and spirals, studded the walls by the thousand and hung in long strings from above. Small round openings, like the portholes of a ship, dotted the opposite side of the cavern in countless scores of horizontal lines; and little door-like apertures opened at regular intervals all along the cavern floor.

Many minutes must have passed while we stood there spellbound. . . .

My companion was standing bemused, near the brink, and I pulled him back. "Better watch out, Phil, or I won't have even your watch to bring to your mother!"

Still like a man in a daze, he wiped a grimy hand over his carrot-colored hair. "Good thing she can't see me now!"

Before I had time to reply, the earth wavered violently once more; distant thunders and detonations burst out with renewed fury. At the same time, a shaft of violet light shot across the cavern with lightning swiftness. Then, in the barest fraction of a second, waves of orange light and of vermilion followed; and while Clay and I stared at each other, the greenish-yellow luminaries all flickered and seemed about to be extinguished. Simultaneously, our ears were struck by a distant blast of sound, a little like the notes of a bugle; and the next instant, as the greenish-yellow lights regained their former brilliance, a scene of startling activity became visible on the cavern floor.

Had we obeyed our hammering hearts, we should have turned and fled; but we did not wish to seem cowards in each other's eyes. We flung ourselves upon the gallery floor, crept to the edge of the abyss, and gazed across, like small boys clandestinely watching a ball game.

2. THE BATTLE

From our vantage point near the cavern roof, we could not follow all that was happening a mile beneath us; however, we did observe more than a little. In the beginning, we were astonished to see the doors at the base of the excavation all thrown open, to admit a multitude of antlike black mites— all of them so minute, in view of their distance, that they might have been insects. To learn the details of their appearance or costume was out of the question. They drew themselves up into precise rectangular formations, each divided into scores of long, mathematically even columns.

"By heaven!" I exclaimed.

"Sure enough, an army!" grunted Clay. "Just see the banners gleaming!"

By straining my eyes, I could distinguish flashes of yellow and purple, as from the waving of battle flags.

"Say, look down there!" my companion broke out a second later, leaning over the edge until I feared he would take a mile-long fall. "There's not one army—there's two!"

At the risk of losing my own balance, I leaned out fully as far as Clay, staring into the dreadful chasm. Just under us was a second army, its innumerable multitudes arrayed in neat rectangles, its banners flashing in vermilion and green.

From opposite sides of the cavern the two great masses of men, each composed of scores of thousands of individuals, were approaching one another with slow and gracefully coordinated movements.

"Where do all those fellows come from?" marveled Clay. "Say, do you know—"

But he was not to complete his sentence; it was as if the entire cavern had burst into flame, as if a thunderstorm of unparalleled fury had flared simultaneously at a hundred points. There came a wave of dazzling white light, which flashed across the cavern on a jagged course and all but blinded us; then, we were smitten by a clap of thunder so severe that our eardrums rang. Almost instantly, other detonations followed, and new lightnings streaked and blazed. At the same time, the ground began to shake once more, and

11

from moment to moment the tremors increased in severity. Now we could understand the source of the earthquakes.

Speechless as deaf-mutes, Clay and I stared at each other. But in his startled eyes I read a message: "Come, let's go!" And one hand was motioning away down the gallery.

I would have followed his suggestion, but my muscles would not obey my will. I quivered, rose to my knees, and then dropped full-length once more. Yet terror could not subdue curiosity; I still gazed down at that fantastic cavern floor, over which the colored lightnings flickered. But now, in place of the armies, multitudes of black specks were strewn pellmell about the cavern floor, in all manner of distorted positions, some of them bunched together in great dark heaps, some clustered amid little new-made crimson patches!

"Do you see?" I exclaimed, when a lull in the thunder permitted conversation.

"Shot to tatters!" Clay said. "Wonder what it was all about."

"Marvelous, anyway, how those lightnings work."

"Marvelous how both sides won!" He snapped back. "Doesn't seem to be much left of either of them!"

While the lightnings still leaped and vaulted through space, crossing and crisscrossing the atmosphere with flames of blue and yellow, there arose a low, regular, distant rumbling.

"What's this coming?" Clay pointed far down the cavern. "Frank! Can you make it out?"

"It's a battleship on wheels."

"No, not one of them—two!" shouted Clay.

Two monster shapes, each as large as super-dreadnoughts, were gliding out of the greenish-yellow glare far to the right. With long, pointed, steel-like prows, tapering sterns, and squat funnels belching smoke and steam, they had much the shape and appearance of warships, except that they displayed no masts or gun turrets. But little dark tubes curving from their sides did look somewhat like guns.

"See the wheels!" yelled Clay, trying to make himself heard against the increasing uproar; and I saw that scores of wheels, each twenty or thirty feet across, were arranged all along the sides of the great machines, bearing them forward with the speed of an ocean liner.

"Seem to be in a hurry!" I yelled back. Clay, no longer able to make his voice heard against the din of the approaching Titans, was nudging my elbow and pointing in great agitation to our left.

From far down the cavern, three more land battleships were rumbling toward us, shooting out flashes of red and white lightning like a challenge, while hastening to meet the other Colossi as though intending a head-on collision.

On and on, the two battle-monsters came, their forms half concealed in puffs and streamers of black smoke. Waving at the stern of one group, we could distinguish banners of yellow and purple, while the other group displayed green and vermilion flags; but otherwise it was hard to tell them apart. On the decks of all the vessels we could see swarms of animated black specks; from the curved tubes at their sides we observed darts of lightning shooting intermittently; and meantime, their rumbling and roaring was as of a thousand locomotives in simultaneous action.

As they drew near one another, there came a prodigious hissing of steam. The five rushing monsters were obscured amid clouds of vapor, through which the blue and yellow lightning flared in innumerable bolts. Our aching ears caught the shock of a concussion so severe that for a second we were stunned; then other shocks, equally severe, as though a mile-high giant were striking blows with a sledge hammer.

Slowly, the din subsided, the wavering ground regained its balance. For a minute we saw nothing; the depths were blanketed in a fuming yellow vapor, which obscured everything like a heavy fog and tormented our nostrils with acrid odors.

Owing to our physical discomfort, we did not know how or when the mists were dissipated. But when at last Clay leaned once more across the cavern edge, he uttered a surprised, "Battle's over! Say, it looks like a tie!"

"Tie?" I echoed, staring toward the pit. "But where under heaven are the fighters?"

"There aren't any more fighters!" mumbled Clay—and this was the literal truth. The landgoing battleships, which had snorted and thundered so violently a few minutes before, were no longer to be seen. The rocky ground, plowed up and torn as by Titanic dredges, had been beaten into ridges and furrows like the waves of a stormy sea; the opposite canyon wall had been wrecked, and great masses of broken boulders were heaped up where the porthole-like openings had stared.

Here and there along the scarred and charred pit-floor,

we saw twisted rods and wires, bent and dented iron plates, contorted coils, broken rods, fragments of wheels and axles.

For a long while we gazed in silence at that desolate battle-field. Then Clay's lip curled in a faintly contemptuous expression. "You know, Frank, these caves must be inhabited by raving lunatics. Thank God, they haven't any atomic weapons. Why, if they had the sense of a two-year-old, they'd know enough not to fight when they'd all be blown to smithereens!"

"Looks that way, doesn't it? But how could we expect to have any wars at all if everyone had the sense of a two-year-old?"

From the cavern walls opposite us, where the little round openings had not been blown away in the recent engagement, a shaft of red lightning leapt, striking not many yards below us. And almost instantly another bolt shot out, and another, and another still, each coming nearer us than the last, while our ears rang with the uproar.

We had been seen and mistaken for enemies.

As we sprang up and away, a deafening crash resounded at our heels, and we knew that the ledge where we had lain had been shattered. The next instant, an even louder crash burst forth, and a huge rock mass, dislodged from the gallery roof, came roaring down almost at our feet.

I darted off into the shelter of one of the many side-galleries, and did not halt even when reaching this relative safety, but kept on at full speed down the vaguely lighted corridor, until at last my pounding heart forced me to stop.

Then, wheeling about, I was swept by new alarm. Where was Clay?

Frenziedly I retraced my footsteps, back to the main corridor where I had last seen Clay, shouting his name. There was no reply. Finally, I entered the corridor and stared out across its greenish-yellow spaces. The gallery was empty.

3. THE CHALK-FACES

For a long, blank moment I stood staring out across that deserted passageway; now that Clay was gone, it was as if the very underpinnings of my world had been torn away.

I began racing up and down. I peered fruitlessly into the shadows of half a score side-galleries; and into each of them I called as loudly as my cracked and broken voice would permit. But still only echoes replied.

I had called into the tenth or eleventh passageway, when an answering yell met my ears—not the voice I sought, but a high-pitched cry in some unknown tongue.

Almost at the same instant, an apparition glided forth amid the dimness of the side-gallery. Picture a man-sized figure, robed from head to foot in black, and with a sable hood, the shape of a fool's cap! Its face was chalky-white, and a toothless mouth gaped as the creature started forward with black-gloved hands extended, that shriek still shrilling from its lips.

I did not take time for further observation. Despite all I had endured, my legs retained their vigor; not for nothing had I been on the track team at college. But as I rushed like a hounded deer along the main gallery, something tripped me, and I pitched head over heels.

Hastily picking myself up, I was about to resume my flight—when I found my path blocked. All about me, at distances of from ten to twenty yards, were dozens of strange beings.

They were riding cross-legged on queer, low cars, of about the size and shape of children's coasters—three or four feet long, a foot high, and a foot wide. Motors buzzed as they darted back and forth, frequently colliding with one another.

Like the one who had started me on my flight, they were all black-clad from crown to heel; they all had snowy-white faces which seemed scarcely human. Their hair, protruding in long tufts from beneath their cone-shaped hats, was either paper-white or gray; their eyes, narrower than those of most men, gave the impression of being not fully open, and were pink or salmon-colored. Their noses were flat and stubby,

their chins weak and almost unnoticeable, while their chests
were so stooped and pinched that I could have believed the
whole lot of them to be consumptives.

Had it not been for the latter features, I might have mistaken them all for women, for they wore long skirts, which
came down well beneath the knees. The impression of fem-
ininity was reinforced by the V-slits in the backs of their
costumes, and the black penciling of their eyebrows, which
were overlooked by little snakelike curves, painted as if for
artistic effect.

Although surrounding me, the creatures kept at a distance
of not less than ten yards, while rolling restlessly back and
forth in their little cars. Several of them carried long, dragon-
shaped banners of green and vermilion, and others bore small,
pistol-like implements, from which every now and then a
lightning shaft flashed toward the ceiling.

Several minutes went by, during which the creatures stared
at me. They jabbered to one another in those peculiar high-
pitched voices so unpleasant to my ears; others pointed at me
with gestures that may have indicated surprise, derision, or
anger. One of them even stepped forth a little, and addressed
me in particularly loud and rasping tones, of which I could
understand nothing.

But when I, in my turn, called out to them as a test, "Who
are you? Where am I?" they answered with a round of such
unpleasant, grating laughter that I resolved to hold my tongue
thenceforth.

I do not know whether the people interpreted my words
as mockery, or were incensed by my failure to answer them
intelligibly; in any case, I could see an expression of hostility
in their salmon-colored eyes. Nevertheless, I was little prepared for their next action. From a rifle-like machine in the
hands of the foremost man, a coil of wire leapt forth; and,
before I realized the intention or had had a chance to evade
it, the coil had fallen over my neck and was tightening about
my shoulders, drawing my arms together against my sides
and binding me like a lassoed steer.

Naturally, I struggled; but the chief effect was to provoke
more laughter. The metal, thick as my index finger, would
not yield to my most frantic efforts.

After a minute or two, my captors began pulling at the
wire. Some of the little coaster-like machines rolled behind
me, and some rolled ahead, but none approached within ten

yards. I was led away down one of the side-galleries like a dog at the end of a leash.

So bewildered was I that for a long while I paid little heed to where we went. I only knew that we were making our way down, down, down, among a multitude of galleries that curved, and curved again, and branched and interbranched with baffling intricacy—galleries illuminated by a greenish-yellow glow from the multitudes of orbs fastened at regular intervals along the walls and ceiling.

After a while, however, I began to take closer note of my surroundings. I remember, for example, catching a glimpse of a huge, rapidly revolving wheel, larger than a barn door, from which a strong draft of cool air was blowing. I saw through a half-closed gateway into a hall filled with machines as high as a five-story building; I was dazzled by flashes of sun-brilliant lights, and once or twice my ears were smitten with thunder blasts. I crossed a bridge over a subterranean torrent, in which I could see half-submerged, illuminated vessels. I passed walls lined with little round lighted windows, beyond which I could distinguish shadowy figures moving: I shuffled along corridors where pipes, coils, and strands of wire ran along the walls for great distances.

Absorbed in these sights, I had regained something of my composure when, coming to the end of a narrow passageway, we found ourselves facing a thoroughfare. Along a gallery fifty or sixty yards across, a multitude of little cars were shooting back and forth with prodigious speed.

None of them was any larger than the tiny machines of my captors; but all were moving with such velocity that it was almost impossible to follow their movements. They seemed to pursue no regular route, but looped and curved at crazy angles, and so many were the near-collisions that it made me dizzy merely to look at the vehicles.

Across this mad avenue my captors set forth with the utmost nonchalance, weaving their way in and out unconcernedly. And I, though I strained back at my wire like a balky hound, was forced to follow. The diabolical little machines came racing toward me from all sides, and none would relax its speed as it approached. I felt one of them flitting just behind me with a rush of wind; another almost scraped the tips of my shoes as it darted in front of me; a third would certainly have ended my days on earth had it not swerved a fraction of an inch just as it was about to destroy me. By the time I had reached the further side, I was near to nervous prostration!

I was just sighing with relief at my deliverance, when there came a loud crash from my rear; glancing back, I saw two of the cars jumbled together in a distorted heap, their drivers sprawled along the cavern floor. One of them, lying motionless, was evidently already beyond help; the second was twisting and groaning miserably. But no one seemed to pay any attention to them.

Fifteen minutes later, we had reached our destination; we emerged into a long, straight cavern, with walls several hundred feet apart and a vaulted ceiling fifty yards high. One of my captors, flinging open a little door at one side, motioned me to enter.

Not being allured by the vague, indistinctly lighted interior, I made no attempt to obey—at which my master seized a long two-pronged pole from the cavern wall and thrust the weapon forward so as to catch me between the prongs. Thus held, I was helpless; and though I roared my resentment, I was shoved through the doorway like a captive beast. The next moment, I heard the heavy hinges rattling shut, and the door slammed in my face.

By the pale greenish-yellow light I found myself in a room about twenty-five feet square, with only one small window, and with a low ceiling that curved down almost to the floor. One or two stone benches and tables, but no chairs, were scattered about this compartment; while, at the further end, half a dozen white-faced and black-robed creatures were cowering.

But when, with the friendliest of intentions, I approached these fellow prisoners, they cringed and withdrew into the remotest corner, trembling, and uttering menacing exclamations.

Being denied their company, I let myself drop upon a stone bench across the room from them. Who were these chalk-faced people? How did they manage to live beneath the earth? Why had no one ever heard of them before? What did they intend to do with me? And what had happened to Clay?

My head was aching, my tongue was growing dry, by the time the prison door opened once more; one of the chalk-faces entered and deposited a bowl of water and some marble-sized purple pills on a table a few yards from me.

To my surprise, my cell-mates all at once made a dash as if to seize these articles, but withdrew in a panic when I stepped forth, and I was left in undisputed possession of the prizes.

At one gulp, I consumed the water; then, feeling somewhat better, took up the purple pills and examined them with interest. As I did so, it flashed over me that these might be poison, intended as an easy means of disposing of us all. What more natural, therefore, than that I should seize the pills and scatter them over the floor?

With wild whoops and cries, my cell-mates leapt after the purple globules, each fighting to be first. Then, as if stricken blind, they began to grope as they drew near the objects, apparently locating them by touch alone.

It was at this point that I made my first discovery about the chalk-faces. They were unable to see things clearly close at hand. My second discovery was that the purple pellets were food. That was evident from the way that my cell-mates, having found them, thrust them eagerly into their toothless mouths and smacked their lips in relish.

Cursing my stupidity, I managed to seize the last of the globules, barely in time to save it from the chalk-faces. It had a nutty taste, though somewhat unpalatable due to the lack of salt. Evidently it was concentrated nourishment of a high quality; I felt a new surge of strength the moment I had consumed it.

Two or three hours after my incarceration, the prison door was shoved violently inward, to admit a troop of ten beings, who had evidently made every effort to appear inhuman. The head of each was enveloped in a triangular mask of steel, which came to a hatchet point in front, and displayed apertures for the eyes, mouth, and nostrils. Their bodies were encased in dark cloth covered with flakes of steel, which clattered as they walked; their feet, which carried long, spike-like spurs both in front and behind, were clothed in iron-plated boots that came almost to the knees; their right hands bore shining weapons, shaped a little like sawed-off shotguns, the ends of which scintillated with flying sparks.

They all stepped forward, their movements so stiff and regular that I had a fleeting suspicion they were animated machines. Their arms swayed up and down, up and down, in perfect time with those of their companions; their feet always left the ground with a peculiar high-swinging motion, like that of prancing horses, although their pace was by no means a prancing one; while the sound of their footsteps reminded me of cavalry trotting.

Having seen Nazi films, it was evident to me that they were soldiers. At a steady pace, they approached my cell-mates, who were shaking and whimpering with dread. Abruptly they halted; their leader pointed to one of the wretches and snapped out an order.

Instantly, the victim was seized by one of the warriors and dragged away, while the whole party left the room at their odd, prancing march.

As the door rattled to a close behind them, my remaining cell-mates all dashed toward the one small window, scuffling and wrestling with one another for a favorable position. Not wishing to be left behind if there was anything to see, I darted toward the window. The effect was as though I were a plague-bearer; the chalk-faces all made way, whining with fear, and retreated to the further end of the room.

Gazing into the broad, high corridor just outside our prison, I saw my late cell-mate being borne to the opposite wall, where he was tied against a stone column shaped like a gallows. Then, while a group of about fifty chalk-faces gathered around, gibbering and gesticulating, one of the soldiers uttered a warning cry; at which the spectators all fell silent; they withdrew to a respectable distance as a curious-looking machine was wheeled onto the scene.

It rested, like a camera, on an iron tripod; it consisted, in the main, of a series of prisms and lenses, of various shapes and colors. Some of these were transparent and but a few inches across, but the foremost was rounded in form, stained a deep opaque blue, and fully a yard in diameter. Behind the lenses were numbers of bulbs, wires, and battery-like tubes; the whole instrument, when in operation, made a constant whirring sound, somewhat like a motion-picture projector.

What interested me most of all, however, was that the light issuing from the foremost lens was not scattered or diffused like most rays; it drew sharply to a focus twenty or twenty-five yards ahead of the machine, making a long cone of violet illumination.

One of the soldiers on the operator's seat turned the violet rays on and off two or three times, as if for practice, then gradually moved the instrument so that it pointed directly toward the victim.

The operator looked through a little glass tube, as if to make sure of his position and distance. He raised his black-gloved hand in an imperious gesture, then took out something that looked like a watch, and gazed at it as if keeping careful count of time. . . .

The next instant, I heard the low, regular whirring of the machines. The cone of violet light shot out, its focus directly at the prisoner's heart. The man drooped, and would have fallen except for the ropes that held him; his face, for an instant, became purplish-red, then turned gray and colorless. . . .

Three or four seconds, and all was over. The violet light no longer played, the whirring sound had ceased. One of the soldiers, whistling a tune, cut the lifeless form free; and the people surged back and forth across the gallery as if nothing had occurred.

The explanation was partly clear: the machine generated energy of some nature, powerful enough to reach the heart and check its action by tearing down the tissues.

Having seen enough for one day, I sank down upon a stone bench, clasping my aching forehead with both hands, and wondering what I had done to fall among the most barbarous race ever known. True, they were advanced scientifically, but would any civilized people execute a man with a death ray? Would they not, rather, resort to humane devices, such as hanging or the electric chair?

While absorbed in these ruminations, I was startled to see the prison door burst open once more, admitting the squad of ten soldiers, who advanced with the same machine-like movements and prancing steps as before, singled out another of my cell-mates, bore the cringing victim away, and promptly executed him by means of the violet ray. Four times in the course of the next hour they returned, and each time withdrew one of my fellow prisoners, who shortly afterwards said farewell to this world.

I wondered what the condemned had done. It was by no means consoling to find myself at length alone in the prison, while the last of my cell-mates was being crumpled by the violet rays.

Would I now be left to myself? No—immediately after disposing of the last chalk-face, the soldiers returned; I saw their leader lift a black-clad hand and point in my direction.

4. HIS ABYSMAL EXCELLENCY, THUNO FLATUM

Had I been a criminal, justly sentenced to the electric chair, my fate would have been less hard to bear. Coolly, with the most matter-of-fact manner, my executioners dragged me out of prison, pulled me at the end of a wire to the stone column that had witnessed the six executions, and, still not approaching me, twisted some heavy iron strands against the column in such a way as to hold me tightly against it.

I saw the black-and-white figures of the spectators crowded at a safe distance, their salmon eyes glittering; I saw the ten soldiers with their hatchet helmets looking on like the creatures of some delirious vision; I saw the death-machine being moved into place, and watched the operator as he peered through the little glass tube as if to make sure of his aim. Then, while I grew limp with fright, the executioner lifted his hand to signify that all was ready. . . .

But at this point my recollections blur. My ears caught a telltale whirring; my eyes beheld the cone of violet light . . . Several seconds—long-protracted seconds—went by. I was aware of a faint warmth, a slight tickling sensation above the heart—and that was all. Then, in a wild rush, hope came flooding back. Was I immune to the effects of the rays?

Suddenly the whirring ceased, the violet ray snapped off, and the spectators' excited cries showed that they shared in my own astonishment.

But was I actually saved? Again I heard the fearful buzzing of the machine; again the cone of violet light pointed toward me; again I felt the tickling sensation in my breast. But I still defied the rays of death.

After the third attempt, I saw the soldiers gathered in a little knot as though in agitated conference. I heard the spectators talking noisily; this hubbub went on for several minutes before, to my unspeakable relief, one of the guards reached out a long forked pole and loosened the wires that bound me.

I felt impulsively at my chest, wondering if I had not been wounded, even though I felt no pain. Then sudden light dawned over me. Beneath my coat, which had been punctured with a little round incision like a bullet hole, I felt a small familiar bulge. From an inner pocket, I drew forth a little leather-covered notebook. A deep, charred perforation, reaching almost through the heavy back cover, showed what had checked the deadly rays.

Had my enemies taken the trouble to search me, I might not have escaped. Only their irrational dread of approaching me could account for this omission! But now, what was to prevent my captors from subjecting me once more to the violet rays?

Evidently the same idea occurred to them. They bound me again with wires shot from one of the machines, forcing me to drop the book, which one of the chalk-faces instantly drew toward him with a pronged pole.

As he could not see clearly at close range, he placed it twenty or thirty feet away, and examined it through binoculars, while one of his companions turned the pages. I do not know what he found to edify him, for all that it contained was some mining notes—along with some printed statistical information, such as the names and population of leading cities, the capitals of states, etc.

At this point, I became aware of the approach of a chalk-face of unusual appearance. He was much taller and thinner than any of his countrymen, being well over six feet in height, and lean in proportion; he bent far forward as he walked. His gray hair fell in long braids and curls from his massive brow; his embroidered robe rippled almost to his ankles; and his face, instead of being clean-shaven like that of his fellows showed a long grizzled beard, neatly parted in the center.

At his approach, the others withdrew, like children before some authoritative adult; while he, not heeding them in the least, pushed his way to the front of the crowd, took out his binoculars and peered at my note-book from a convenient distance.

As he did so, I could see his little reddish eyes beaming enthusiastically. He let out a whoop of joy, and rushed toward my notebook. Approaching it, he had even more trouble than his kinsmen in seeing near at hand. However, he finally managed to locate it, and, hugging it to his side as if it were some rare art treasure, uttered another cry of delight.

The next moment, I noticed his eyes fastened upon me, and I felt friendliness in his glance; for the first time since arriving in these nether depths, I had found a defender. I realized that I, personally, interested him less than did my note-book; but I could have kissed his hand when he motioned to my captors, speaking sharply and angrily, and they set me free once more.

No sooner was I released from the wires than my rescuer shrilled an order, and several of the little coast-like cars were wheeled up. I was motioned to take my place on one of them, and upon refusing, was pitched on with a two-pronged pole. It was clear that any attempt to escape would be severely treated, so I lay on the car at full-length, clinging to a little board projecting in front, instead of squatting with crossed legs, in the manner of the natives. How they laughed to see me take this position, amazed that I appeared ignorant of the steering mechanism! But they solved the difficulty by hitch-ing my machine with a wire to another, which forthwith dragged it away.

The ride that followed did not last more than ten minutes. We roared through tunnels, lurched around curves, shot across causeways and bridges, and raced along avenues where other cars shot past in a gray whirl of speed. Finally, we halted—so abruptly that I was pitched forward off my perch, and was only saved from serious injury by falling on my friend, who drove the car ahead of mine.

Not being versed in the native language, I did not know what epithets of abuse he used; infuriated though he was, I could see that his first thought was for my notebook, which he still clutched. Finding this unharmed, he seemed to be consoled.

We were now joined by half a dozen more chalk-faces, including several soldiers who had followed us on other cars; and the whole party, without delay, started down a brilliantly lighted gallery toward a great shining hall. As always, most of the chalk-faces kept at a distance from me, some of them trotting half a dozen yards behind, and others as many yards ahead; but my rescuer, surprisingly, seemed willing to walk at my side.

As we drew near the hall, my companions slackened their pace; and when we had come within a stone's throw of the entrance, I was startled to see a row of soldiers, their faces hidden in triangular helmets, their right hands clutching pikes twenty feet high. They all stood stiff as stone, and made no response to our salutes; in fact, at first I supposed them to be statues.

However, after one of our attendants had spoken, slipping

a little something into their hands, two of the soldiers moved aside a few feet, making room for us to pass; and we entered the hall beyond.

I was now surprised to see my companions drop to their knees, and move forward on all fours, in a groveling attitude which I could not be persuaded to imitate until convinced by a sharp cuff on the small of the back. Even my protector had fallen into a most ungainly and unbecoming posture. Watching his lanky form, as he crept forward foot by foot on hands and knees, I could not restrain a burst of laughter, which cost me a second and even more severe cuff on the back.

What was it that filled the chalk-faces with such humility? Had they entered the shrine of a god, or the throne room of their king? After a moment, I accepted the latter explanation. The walls of the hall—which was at least a hundred yards across—were emblazoned with multitudes of brilliant white, red, and yellow lights. Enormous, dragon-shaped banners of green and vermilion hung from the high fretted ceilings, interspersed with long strings of swords, pikes, and helmets. In the center, on a raised platform of polished red sandstone, sat the most remarkable individual I had ever seen.

He may have been four feet high, but I doubt it; his lean and wizened frame may have been as stout as that of an eight-year-old, but I doubt it. The legs were little more than two dangling sticks; his arms were scarcely better developed. His head was bald, his mouth toothless, and his fingers without nails. His eyes were covered with instruments like binoculars, through which, apparently, he could see only with difficulty; his ears were hidden by a mass of wires, and by black projections like telephone receivers. His nostrils were encased in rubber-like tubes, connecting with steel tanks—which, as I later learned, contained oxygen. His mouth, likewise, was fitted with breathing tubes, which I saw him remove only in order to talk (a feat he accomplished by means of a megaphone).

In fact, the poor creature seemed to have scarcely one of his natural faculties intact!

Unlike his fellows, he was robed not in black, but in resplendent green and saffron, with a purple crest upon his hairless pate, and a string of huge rubies dangling about his neck. All about him, in a gleaming circle, a row of large mirrors was displayed; and through these he was feasted with a constant view of himself, and could catch every turn and nod and twist of his imperial countenance. Furthermore, other mirrors, spaced at intervals about the room, caught and magnified the reflections of the ones nearest him; so that, in no matter what direction you looked, you were sure to see his image.

Doubtless it was appropriate that the greater part of the room should contain nothing at all except the reflection of the central dignitary. But just around him, twenty attendants stood in waiting on the sandstone platform; and whenever he made a move or a gesture—were it only to smooth out his dress or scratch the back of his neck—at least half of them would rush up to serve him. I well remember their consternation when their master bent forward and sneezed. For a moment, I thought I was witnessing a riot as the twenty attendants, as one man, leapt forward to readjust the nose-tubes, which had been blown out of place.

All this I observed while my companions and I crept up to the throne. Why should the chalk-faces, absurd as they were, do reverence to such a monarch? But realizing that there is no accounting for political tastes, I remained crouching in a deferential attitude after we had finally halted twenty yards from the throne.

For at least half an hour we remained on all fours, miserably waiting—at least, I was miserable. During all this time, the sovereign remained seated in a sort of dreamy trance. It seemed to be the rule among the chalk-faces that subjects should not speak until spoken to; hence we might have remained stooping there all day, and still not have gained an audience, had the dignitary not caught sight of me and become interested.

So interested was he, in fact, that he rose from his seat and tottered to the edge of the platform—a distance of fully six feet, which he traversed with the utmost difficulty, while three attendants supported him on each side. Then, for at least a minute, he stared at me intently through his binoculars, until, exhausted from the effort, he had to be carried to his chair and fanned back to life.

This process consumed at least ten minutes; at length the sovereign, restored by the fanning of his servants, and strengthened by hypodermic injections, was revived sufficiently to be able to speak through the megaphone which a vassal lifted to his mouth. Of course, I did not know what he said. The words were high-pitched and squeaky, and rasped upon me like a file; but the effect was most welcome. All of us were able to rise to our feet.

Now my protector, after a flourish and a low bow, waved my notebook high in air for all to see, and launched into speech. The words came out in a rattling torrent; many minutes went by with scarcely a pause for breath, while all the other chalk-faces made hardly an effort to conceal their yawns. At last even the monarch, apparently, could endure it no longer. He lifted his arm in a gesture of command, motioned for the megaphone, and snapped out two short words—which instantly put an end to my friend's discourse.

Not until much later did I learn that the ruler had granted everything asked, but the speech, as I afterwards read it in the court records, ran as follows:

"Lord High Dictator Thuno Flatum, sovereign of the great empire of Wu and illustrious ruler of the Underworld and the Overworld, I Professor Tan Torm, prostrate myself before you! Long may your distinguished might endure! Long may your power cause the nations to shake! I come to you today on a momentous mission, and I trust you will let no thought of my personal unworthiness deter you from that just decision for which you are so rightly renowned. Know, O Thuno Flatum, that this day a stranger of queer and unprepossessing appearance has been found in our midst. His dark skin and gray eyes proclaim him to be a member of one of those colored races of which ancient traditions tell. But he was at first mistaken for a spy, sent out against us by our enemy Zu in the current war. This view was reinforced by the fact that he was found in the Scouting Galleries, just above Black Ravine, where the forces of Your Abysmal Excellency have this day won such a glorious victory. Hence he was sentenced to be liquidated, in accordance with that famous maxim, '*In wartime, kill first, and investigate afterwards.*'

"But, as fortune would have it, I arrived in time to save him. Your Abysmal Excellency will observe the curious little book which I carry in my hand; this proves him to be not a spy, but a creature of some outside race, who arrived in some manner beyond our imagining. It is preposterous, of course, to suppose that he came from the Overworld—which, as our scientists have conclusively proved, is incapable of supporting intelligent life—since all but the lowest of living things would be instantly killed by the sunlight and fresh air. But may he not have come from caverns deep down in the earth's center, where we have never penetrated?

"This is my theory, Your Abysmal Excellency; and it is

supported by the queer writing in his book, which I take to be the hieroglyphics of the crude and undeveloped race of which he is a member. As a philologist, I cannot but be interested; and as a student of primitive calligraphy, I consider that here is an unparalleled opportunity for scholarly research. So I request, Abysmal Excellency, that you permit me to take him to my own home, where I will care for him and will attempt—in the event that his mind be capable of absorbing a few simple facts—to educate him in the rudiments of our language, so as better to study his habits in the interest of science. I will deliver a full report, in not less than three octavo volumes, before the Royal Institute of Anthropological Abnormalities, and meanwhile will put up a bond to take every reasonable care of the prisoner, and not let him bite anyone, or escape. . . ."

Such was but the opening of Tan Torm's speech, which continued in this vein for thirty pages.

5. THE PEOPLE OF THE CAVERNS

The home of Professor Tan Torm was typical of the so-called "Second Class" citizen of the country of Wu. It was composed of five or six small rooms, excavated out of solid rock, and opening on one of the numerous side-galleries. There were no windows; light was provided by the yellowish-green electric bulbs, while a constant supply of air was forced in through whirling, fanlike devices located in little orifices near the front door. All in all, the Professor's abode was comfortable enough, although I could never accustom myself to the stone chairs and tables, the stone beds without pillows, or the grotesque hangings and adornments—small likenesses of swords, helmets, and land-battleships—which constituted the native idea of art.

The family of the Professor included his wife, Tan Tal, and his three daughters, Loa, Moa, and Noa. On first entering the house, I assumed that Tan Tal, the mother, was the most youthful of the girls; while Loa, the last-born daughter, struck me as undoubtedly the parent. This mistake was only natural, due to the idea of beauty entertained by the ladies of Wu.

For it was their opinion—in which the men seemed to share —that the supreme mark of a woman's loveliness was her wrinkles, and that the more wrinkles she boasted—particularly around the eyes and on the neck—the more alluring was her appearance. Hence all the damsels used to spend hours a day with wrinkle-producing creams, permanent "wrinkle-wavers," and other devices to create creases in their naturally smooth countenances. Only the old and matronly women, who were past the stage of trying to shine before their husbands, could afford to let their features unwrinkle themselves.

It was for this reason that Loa—who, as I was later told, had barely reached seventeen—impressed me as being of advanced years. She was rendered all the more hideous by the cream-colored paint with which she daubed her lips, and by the fact that her eyelashes, in accordance with the native custom, had been shaved away. Yet in the estimation of the chalk-faces, Loa was a beauty!

While the men wore skirts, the women all went around in trousers. All females, above the age of four or five, wore loose, pajama-like pantaloons of various colors; and it was considered indecent for a lady to appear in any other costume.

I was regarded with contempt, because my trousers were considered unbecoming for a gentleman. Only after Professor Tan Torm had come to the rescue with one of his old black skirts was I able to appear in respectable society.

I am sure that any of the local youths would have envied me the privilege of being instructed in the native language and institutions by the beautiful Loa. Professor Tan Torm, of course, supervised my education; but he was so absorbed in his researches into the roots of extinct verbs that he could not give me more than a few minutes each day.

I must acknowledge that Loa took her task conscientiously enough—even though her first efforts were not to teach me the language, but to teach me how to pencil my eyebrows, whiten my cheeks and lips, and bleach my hair, so as to conform to the native idea of male decorum. Failing in these efforts, she resigned herself with a sigh to the inevitable; yet from the way in which she glanced at me from time to time, I could see that my charms, such as they were, had had too much of an effect on her.

But let me pass from this subject for the present. First, there was the necessity of studying the native language; fortunately, I made rapid steps in this direction, for Loa was a capable teacher. Within two or three weeks, I could exchange elementary ideas; within a month, I could conduct a brief conversation. In less than three months, I was able to carry on an extended colloquy with any member of Tan Torm's household, and would not miss more than an occasional word, due to the limits of my vocabulary.

The Underworld, I learned, was composed of the twin countries of Wu and Zu, and reached for hundreds of miles in all directions. It underlay not only most of Nevada, but much of Utah, Arizona, and adjoining states. This whole vast universe, comprising a multiplicity of great caverns and smaller connecting gallaries, was inhabited by a population variously estimated as between eight and ten millions—all of them chalk-faced, light-haired and salmon-eyed, like the ones I had already seen. Neither Loa nor her father could tell me how long they had dwelt underground; their written records dated back thousands of years. While there were traditions that once they had lived in a land of blue skies and open air, from which they had been driven to escape annihilation in warfare, such tales had never been verified by historical research. It was generally held that human life had originated in caverns below, and that, as population multiplied, men had excavated new caverns to take care of the surplus millions.

In fact, it would have been impossible for the chalk-faces to appear above ground unless they wore heavy metal suits, like those of undersea divers. Unprotected, their white skins having lost all pigment in the course of the ages, exposure to the sun would be fatal. Hence their belief—which scientists had confirmed by means of elaborate mathematical proofs—that no intelligent life could endure above ground; and hence the fact that none of them had ever been observed by our race.

But how did the millions of Wu and Zu manage to preserve their sub-surface life? How contrive to eat, breathe, and clothe themselves?

The secret, as I had early surmised, was to be found in the prodigious scientific development of the Underworld. I do not exaggerate when I say that the people were far in advance of our race; they had evolved mechanical formulae and devices of which we have not the remotest conception. As an engineer by profession, I was naturally much interested in this phase of their growth; and while I was unable to study or understand all their numerous contrivances, yet I could understand enough to stir me with admiration.

I shall not take time, at this point, to dwell upon all their elaborate appliances—which, indeed, would require a separate volume even for their enumeration. I shall begin, therefore, by telling of the manufacture of food and clothing, which was conducted on principles I had never before considered possible.

Let me say, by way of explanation, that my food in the Professor's house was comprised in part of purple capsules and in part of a stringy, fibrous substance reminding me of seaweed. I was told, however, that the wealthier classes occasionally enjoyed delicacies such as fish from subterranean rivers, and mushrooms grown in specially prepared cellars; though if Professor Tan Torm could afford these luxuries, he did not waste them on a barbarian such as myself.

My clothes, likewise, were of a substance I could not recognize—a woven material a little like hemp and yet clearly not hemp, for it was not quite so coarse. But the fibers did not resemble those of linen, cotton, silk, or wool. The answer, as I learned from Loa, was that the native clothing, and also the food, was manufactured synthetically. From the most ordinary chemicals—oxygen and hydrogen as contained in water, carbon as contained in carbon dioxide or coal, nitrogen as found in the air, the sulphur and phosphorus of the mines—they would create compounds resembling natural organic products.

The simplest of all to manufacture were starch and sugar, and a fiber like the cellulose of plants. For these, all that was required was a brilliant lamp, imitating the qualities of sunlight; a chemical cell which utilized the lamp rays as the chlorophyll of the vegetable kingdom utilizes the solar beams; and an adequate supply of water and carbon. Thus the people might obtain all the carbohydrates they required for the table, and all the fibers needed for weaving into paper and clothes; for, since cellulose constitutes the main ingredient of cotton and other vegetable fabrics, it was possible to produce a synthetic equivalent of the garments worn in the world above.

More difficult was the problem of the nitrogenous foodstuffs; but here again the ingenuity of the chalk-faces had proved equal to the task. I was never able to understand by what process they had succeeded in combining nitrogen with oxygen, hydrogen, carbon and other substances to form albumin; but it is certain that this is precisely what they did, fusing the elements by means of an electric current and several catalytic agents, whose nature I was unable to learn.

Let me say, at this point, that I did make every effort to find out; but the formula was the carefully guarded secret of National Food Producers, Unlimited. It was forbidden by law to tell the people too much about the food they ate.

In the field of the power system by which the chalk-faces kept their factories running, excavated and illuminated their galleries, and conducted their warfare, I was better able to satisfy my curiosity. I was told that they generated electrical energy in part from the flow of underground rivers, and in part by means of a chemical discovery made so long ago that no one remembered the inventor. This was the compound known as Mulflar, an explosive.

Once again, I could not discover the formula, for this was

the private property of National Power Producers, Exclusive, who had long ago succeeded in passing legislation prohibiting themselves from making the facts public. The general principles, however, were well known: Mulflar was made by the union of nitrogen, phosphorus, magnesium, and sulphur with carbon, hydrogen, and one or two other elements in a compound both simply and easily produced. Its distinctive feature was the unstability of its atoms, which would disintegrate and explode upon the slightest shock or upon the application of a spark, releasing a prodigious amount of energy through the conversion of that active element, hydrogen, unto the chemically inert helium.

So great was the explosive power of Mulflar that a single gram, properly directed, was capable of blowing a hundred pounds of iron to the height of half a mile. Naturally, so dangerous a substance had to be carefully controlled; and though accidents sometimes did occur—resulting in the occasional loss of a hundred lives—in general, it was highly adaptable to industrial uses. Shot off in small quantities in cannon-like tubes of specially prepared steel, it was used to set great dynamos into action, and consequently to furnish the larger part of the electricity indispensable to life. It was the energy of Mulflar, passed into storage batteries, that made it possible to run those coaster-like little cars with which I had had such a frightening experience; it was the energy of Mulflar that kept the lights and the ventilation in operation, ran the food and clothing factories, and pumped fresh water into pipes throughout the length and depth of the land.

But, at the same time, Mulflar accounted for the deadliness of the native warfare; Mulflar had produced the lightnings that Clay and I had watched in such fascinated horror; Mulflar had supplied the motive power for the land-battleships, and had blown those gigantic machines to tatters.

Hardly an hour went by but that I thought of Philip Clay; consequently, as soon as I could speak the native language, I asked about my friend.

Both Professor Tan Torm and his daughter looked astonished when they understood my question. "Great caverns! You say there were two like you? I only wish there were. That would double the opportunities for verification of my theories."

"Another like you?" queried Loa, in milder tones; and then burst into laughter. "Why, that's just too silly for words! I'm sure there couldn't be two like you in the whole deep world!"

Not knowing whether or not to take this as a compliment, I said nothing, while the Professor continued:

"My dear friend, if another man like you had been found anywhere in Wu, we would know of it instantly. The news would be flashed from end to end of the country—just as your own arrival has been."

"My friend wasn't *exactly* like me," I explained. "He was taller, and his hair was red—"

For the first time in my experience, the Professor bent nearly double with laughter, his long ungainly frame rocking back and forth in mirth. It seemed minutes before he and Loa could suppress their merriment.

"His hair—red?" echoed Tan Torm. "Red? Red, you say? My dear man, who ever heard of red hair?"

"You don't mean green, do you?" interjected Loa. "Or maybe purple, orange, or lavender?"

And she and her father, after assuring me that no red-haired man had ever been seen before in all the land of Wu, went off again into spasms of laughter.

6. THE WAY OF WU

While I was questioning Professor Tan Torm and his family as to the Underworld, they were equally eager in asking about my own land.

Naturally, they were anxious to know where I had come from, and how I had arrived; but since they had decided that I had escaped from some cavern far below them, my story met with incredulous smiles. Their attitude was about what ours would be if some stranger should assert that he came from the depths of the sea. "No use trying to deceive us!" they cried reprovingly. "The Overworld is not capable of supporting human life!"

And then curiously they asked, "Are the people where you come from all colored like you?"

"Colored?" I flung back, a little irritated. "I'm white!"

"What an idea!" they jeered, pointing to my rosy-complexioned face. "Great caverns! You call that white? Why, you're pink!"

Loud was the laughter that convulsed the family group.

"If *you're* white, then what are we?" demanded Loa.

I had nothing to say in reply.

"My dear young man," consoled Professor Tan Torm, "do not let the matter of your origin grieve you. We know that birth is not a matter of choice, and if nature has made you a member of an inferior race, at least it speaks well for you that you could rise to join us."

"But I didn't rise to join you!" I insisted. "I descended! I fell into your world by accident, through a fissure caused by the shocks of your warfare."

This explanation, however, was ignored, while the members of the family exchanged significant glances. It was Tan Tal, the charming wife of Tan Torm, who put the next question:

"Where you come from, is there only one country? Or is there more than one, so as to give you someone to fight with?"

"Oh, we're not at all limited in that way," I declared. "We've simply no end of lands to fight with."

At this announcement, the three young daughters of the family tittered uncontrollably.

"Why, how funny!" laughed Loa.

"How confusing!" giggled Moa.

"How absurd!" roared Noa. "Then how do you know which one to fight first?"

Professor Tan Torm, unlike his daughters, had been listening with an unsmiling solemnity. "That is an excellent idea, young man—to divide yourselves into many countries. It is plain that even the barbarians have ideas. Down here, you see, we have only two nations: Wu and Zu. Hence we are much handicapped, from the military point of view. They say that only this year our Secretary of National Offense— poor fellow!—was driven out of his mind to find a plausible reason for declaring war on Zu. However, if we had had some other country to oppose, there would have been no problem at all."

"Yes, it is so, Father," agreed Loa, who by this time had ceased laughing. "Why not recommend to Dictator Thuno Flatum that we split up into several countries?"

"Excellent!" concurred Tan Tal. "Then we could go to war to defend the rights of small nations!"

"But I don't quite understand," I put in. "You're talking as if war is a good thing. Up in our world, we call it a curse!"

"A curse?" echoed all the members of Tan Torm's family, amid an uproar of laughter. "A curse? Mighty abysses! What sort of a world do you have!"

"Don't let anyone here catch you saying that!" warned the Professor, scowling. "If one of the Official Overhears heard you, you'd be courtmartialed!"

"What are the Overhears?"

No one attempted to answer, so I assumed that the Overhears were members of a secret police whose duty it was to overhear and report unpatriotic remarks of their fellow citizens. What I had already observed should have led me to assume, too, that these people considered warfare a great good—but the utter strangeness of things around me often kept me from making logical connections between familiar elements. My guess about the Overhears was right.

"There's no use talking," mused Tan Tal, shaking her head sadly, "the savagery of the colored races is unquenchable. To think they're actually opposed to warfare!"

"It's so unenlightened of them!" condemned Loa.

"So disgusting!" jeered Moa.

"So barbarous!" groaned Noa. "Really, they must still be in the Stone Age!"

"You see, my dear young man," explained the Professor, turning to me not unkindly, "we live in an age of reason. Reason and science—these are the two features of our life, and both of these tell us that man is a fighting animal. Biology assures us that he was created with the instinct of aggression, which is necessary for the sake of self-preservation. Psychology declares that all the instincts planted in him by nature must be satisfied. Accordingly, men satisfy their instinct of self-preservation by destroying one another. That fact was demonstrated long ago by the world's leading military psychologist, the great philosopher Yil Zom."

Tan Tal once more lifted her voice. "Besides, there is another reason. If we didn't fight, think of the loss to industry! Think of all the millions invested in Mulflar Works and land-battleship factories! Why, if we didn't have any war, all this investment would be wasted."

"Yes, and my stocks in Mulflar Products, Amalgamated, couldn't possibly maintain their present high of 311!" said the Professor.

Taking advantage of a gap in the conversation, I asked, "What's the present war all about, Professor Tan Torm? What is the issue, the principle behind it?"

"Issue? Principle behind it?" snorted Tan Torm. "What makes you think there is any issue, any principle behind it? We're fighting for the national honor—and, certainly, there is no principle behind that!"

The Professor paused, energetically stroking his two-pointed beard and glaring at me as though I had been guilty of some offense against decency. "There has to be an *official reason* for the war, of course," he resumed, more mildly. "In this case, we were driven to our wit's ends, and couldn't think of anything better than the old Nullnull dispute."

"What's the Nullnull dispute?"

The five chalk-faces all stared at me a little blankly, as if incredulous. However, the Professor condescendingly explained: "On the borderline between Wu and Zu is the province of Nullnull. This is composed of a series of desert caverns, a dozen miles long and about half as wide. They say that once it was valuable land, containing lakes, streams, and rich ore deposits. However, it has been so shot to pieces that no one lives there now, and it is worthless except as a place to fly the national flag. It is therefore highly coveted by both Wu and Zu.

"In the course of the last thousand years, it has changed hands a hundred and nineteen times, and every time it has been recaptured there has been an excuse for another war—for of course the citizens of the defeated land could not be content to have Nullnull wrenched away from them. Thus the military ardor of both countries has been kept at boiling point, and we have had no trouble in advancing our Military Birth Extension Program."

"Military Birth Extension Program?" I murmured expectantly.

"Exactly what the name implies! In order to keep a war going, what do we need most of all, besides money and ammunition? Naturally, man power! But present-day warfare is so efficient that man power does not last long. It is estimated that the military turnover is seventy-five per cent a year."

"Just what is military turnover?"

"The percenatage of men turned over to the army of the immortals."

"You mean, the percentage killed?"

Tan Torm and the four ladies all glared at me as though I had committed an impiety. The Professor stroked his beard in indignation; the mouths of Loa, Moa, and Noa opened wide with horror.

"Killed? Killed, young man?" thundered Tan Torm. "Never use that word in connection with war! It is not permitted! It is illegal, unpatriotic! No one is *ever* killed in war! Millions are sent to the Blessed Caverns, or converted into deathless champions, or become the Unknown Hero! But no one is ever killed. That is forbidden by law."

"Young man," remonstrated Tan Tal, "remarks like yours are enough to ruin morale."

"If we didn't know you spoke in ignorance, sir, we would have you examined by the Intelligence Department, which would most likely have you executed for speaking without a license!" declared the Professor.

After a moment, however, he seemed softened by my contrite expression; and, regaining his good humor, continued:

"I was going to explain about our Military Birth Extension Program. The idea is that all families should have as many children as possible—sons, so that they may go down to fight for their country, and daughters, so that they may bear more sons to go down to fight for their country. All couples married for ten years or over are required to pay a tax for every child which they have less than seven. But for every child above the seventh, they receive a bonus. The system works so well that we are able to keep our population stationary."

"Stationary? Why, at that rate, it ought to double every generation!"

"It would—except for the military turnover. As it happens, our boys are all enlisted in the army's reserve corps at the age of six, and from that time forth are trained for the next war. So rigorous is the discipline that fifty per cent never reach sixteen. This insures the survival of the fittest.

"At sixteen, the surviving youths are enrolled in the active army, and are sent to the front to face the boys of Zu. They are then offered the hope of retiring as veterans at eighteen, if they should reach that age. But fifteen out of sixteen go over to the Blessed Caverns."

I was about to comment, but refrained, for fear of breaking some penal law.

"Besides being profitable, it is a great honor to have many children," continued the Professor, with zest. "Mothers are given an honorary brass crescent for every son born to them; and fathers receive an honorary crescent of silver. Immediately upon the death"—here Tan Torm paused and coughed in great embarrassment—"pardon me, immediately upon the turnover of a son, the mother and father each receive another honorary crescent. It is this that makes the Birth Extension Program such a succeess."

"Well, Professor, you yourself don't seem to have starred in that line," I remarked, with a side glance at Loa, Moa, and Noa, who surprised me by averting their eyes and sighing. "With only three daughters to your credit—"

"Three daughters?" bellowed Tan Torm, his long black-gloved hand shaking. "And what, pray, of my five sons?"

"Yes, what of our five sons?" echoed Tan Tal, wiping a tear from the corner of one eye.

"Well, what of them?"

"They have all gone to the Blessed Caverns!" sighed the Professor.

"I have five extra crescents for the dear boys!" confided Tan Tal, wiping a second tear from her eye. "Poor darlings! The oldest was just seventeen when he—when he was turned over. I shall always be proud of their gallantry."

"I, too!" said Tan Torm. "It shall be a lifelong source of gratification to look at my five extra crescents, which shall redound to my honor forever."

"*Your* honor?" I broke out. "Who was it, then, that died?"

"Something in me died forever when they—when they were turned over," said the Professor.

Tan Tal meanwhile, with all the suppressed fury of outraged motherhood, was glaring at me as if to devour me whole. "Barbarian! What makes you think they died? They shall live forever in our memory! They shall endure in the annals of their country! They shall live here—here, in the shrine of my breast!"

So speaking, she smote the designated part of her anatomy a blow severe enough to do her physical injury.

"They shall live forever—here in the shrine of my breast!" thundered the Professor, following suit.

I decided to change the topic. "Did you say all the boys of Wu are enlisted in the army? Are there no exceptions?"

"Naturally, there are! All sons of Second and Third Class citizens must go to war, but sons of First Class citizens are exempted."

"Who are the First Class citizens?"

"Why, haven't I told you of our three classes? The division is an ancient one, and is the basis of our social life. The Third Class, which is the most numerous, is sometimes also called the Hungry Class. Its members are notable for doing all the country's hard work, and are so busy they often do not get enough to eat. The people of this caste are prohibited from thinking, lest thought lead to revolt. Above them is the Second or Sedentary Class, to which I have the honor of belonging—its members usually get enough to eat, hence a mild amount of thought is permissible, so long as it doesn't give birth to unlicensed speech. But over us all is the First or Mirror Class, which makes up a little under forty-six one hundredths of one per cent of the population, and owns ninety-eight per cent of the country."

"Why do you call them the Mirror Class?"

"Because, like Thuno Flatum, they never tire of looking at themselves in mirrors. This, of course, is only proper in the class that rules us."

"But I thought Thuno Flatum ruled you."

"Thuno Flatum is the head of the Mirror Class. He has been chosen by the Mirror Class as their leader," continued

Tan Torm, "since he is considered the strongest of them all. In other words, his senses, legs, and lungs are the most atrophied."

This was a bit confusing, for all the totalitarian logic I had just heard.

"You see," he explained, "for ages the Mirror Class has prided itself upon its pure blood. None of its members, under pain of death, has ever been permitted to intermarry with a Second or Third Class citizen. The result of this long interbreeding has been a distinctive type, unlike us low-grade people. Thanks to their lives of luxury, and their constant use of wheeled vehicles, the Mirrors—or Masters, as they are sometimes called—have all but forgotten how to use their legs, which have become thin and shriveled. In the same way, since they have never filled their lungs by exercise or labor, their breathing apparatus has almost withered away. Since they have rarely used their eyes or ears, these organs, too, have become worthless without artificial aid.

"All these qualities are signs of superiority—or of 'green blood,' as aristocracy is called among us. That Master whose lungs are the frailest, whose legs are the feeblest, and whose vision is the dimmest is chosen to lead the country, since the purity of his lineage is the most unquestioned."

Despite my attempt to understand, I committed a gross diplomatic blunder. "I don't see why you stand for it," I blurted out. "I don't see why you let these frail little Masters rule you, own most of the property, and be excused from fighting."

It was a minute before any of them was able to find speech. "Great caverns!" gasped Loa at length, her features more wrinkled than ever as she made a grimace of disgust. "I didn't know we had a revolutionary right here in our own home!"

"Yes, a poisonous revolutionary!" cried Moa. "Who would have believed it!"

"The next thing," exclaimed Noa, "he'll be demanding the single standard in justice!"

"Or an end to two-faced politics!" contributed Tan Tal, glowering at me.

"This is serious indeed!" conceded the Professor. "Of course, allowances must be made for barbarians. You can't expect to civilize them in a minute. We'll take him down to-morrow to the Commissioner of Public Thought, and make him swallow the Oath of Fidelity. After that, if he makes any more disloyal statements, he will have to take the responsibility."

"Good! Very good!" cried the ladies. "We should have done that long ago!"

"And what's the Oath of Fidelity?"

"You'll find out, young man, after you've swallowed it!" snapped the Professor. "And now you've had enough of my time for one day! I must get back to my researches on the history of the comma in ancient literature!"

7. THE OATH OF FIDELITY

On the following day, Professor Tan Torm took me to visit the Commissioner of Public Thought. Or, rather, on the following "wake"; for the chalk-faces, not having the guidance of the sun, divide time into periods of about twelve hours each, which are known alternately as "sleeps" and "wakes."

As this was the first time I had left the Professor's house in months, I strode along at his side with great glee as he led me through the tortuous thoroughfares. Several times, I narrowly missed being felled by one of the small coaster-like vehicles or "scoots"; but despite such near-mishaps, I kept up my good spirits until we had reached our destination—a long, gloomy chamber where fifty chalk-faces were already waiting in line.

"The Commissioner's headquarters are always crowded," stated the Professor, as we took our places at the foot of the procession. "You see, all Second and Third Class citizens are required to swallow the Oath of Fidelity twice a year."

The first in line, having finished his business, passed out a gleaming bit of brass, which was promptly rung up on a cash register by a little chalk-face seated at a table.

For over an hour we remained standing in line; and, to amuse himself during the interval, Tan Torm read to me in loud tones the various signs and placards that hung about the room—signs and placards which I was not yet able to decipher.

"*Lower-class citizens should be seen and not heard. And the less seen the better.*" Then he commented, "That is a maxim dating back thousands of years to our greatest lawgiver, Tith Wyt.

"*A little thought is a dangerous thing,*" continued Tan Torm, turning back to the signs, "*and much thought is impossible. Therefore the ideal citizen will live in a state of sublime thoughtlessness.*

"That is a rule we always do our best to follow," he explained with a boastful smile. "It is the first of the Brass

Rules of Conduct, brass being our most sacred metal—more holy even than silver.

"But I suppose it's useless to try to inculcate such high principles into the barbarian mind," he meditated. "However, here's the second Brass Rule." And he read: "*Thoughtlessness is the best policy. It insures one the respect of one's superiors, the confidence of one's equals, and a successful career in business or politics.*"

Seeing that I had no comment to make, my guide proceeded to the Third Brass Rule: "*Thoughtlessness is next to godliness. A thoughtless mind and soul are the purest creation of the divine. He who thinks not will be content. He who thinks not will spend no time on vain revolt. He who thinks not will never suffer from headaches.*"

There were eleven other Brass Rules, all of which the Professor read with gusto; but my attention had wandered, and I scarcely heard what he said. My mind was far away; I was thinking of Clay. . . .

I was awakened from my reveries by hearing a voice snap, "Next!" I was now first in line.

A scowling little individual sat before me at a stone table, with a cash register as tall as a grandmother's clock towering above him. "Well? What is it?"

"This is my protégé," explained the Professor, coming forward. "Being a barbarian, he knows little of our laws, and I therefore thought it best to give him the Oath of Fidelity before it was too late."

"That's all very well, but who's going to pay?"

"I'll attend to that," agreed Tan Torm. "As a member of the teaching profession, I'm allowed a discount."

"Very well! All accounts strictly cash!" And then, while the Professor muttered, "Fidelity rates come high this year," the official reached for a long roll of paper printed with minute characters. He read aloud from across the room by means of binoculars, hastily, and in mumbling tones; I could distinguish not a word.

Having finished, he thrust the paper forward, pushed a pen into my hand, and directed, "Sign here!"

Although not well versed in the native handwriting, I was able to make a mark that passed for my signature.

With a sigh of relief, I had turned away, when I heard the official's voice ringing out behind me: "Wait a minute! You've forgotten to swallow the Oath!"

I wheeled about, and saw that the paper I had just signed was being rolled into a little pellet in the official's hands.

"Here! Swallow this!" he ordered, tossing it to me after it had been reduced to the size and shape of a marble.

"Swallow it?"

Several persons behind me in line were tittering.

"Do as the man says!" shrilled the Professor's voice in my ear. "What use is the Oath of Fidelity if you don't swallow it—and swallow it whole?"

I reached for the pellet, and regarded it suspiciously. It was as hard and unappetizing as a chip of granite.

"What are you waiting for?" demanded the official. "Don't you want to swallow it? Will we have to call a recruiting sergeant and force it down your throat?"

Realizing that he was in earnest, I lifted the pellet toward my lips; it had an odor of overripe cheese. And so once more I hesitated.

"Great caverns! I suppose we'll have to force it down your throat after all!" threatened the official.

I thrust the Oath into my mouth, but not so easily could I gulp it down. The seconds that followed were among the most miserable of my existence, the Oath of Fidelity caught, and would not go up or down.

They tell me that my face went blue in the ensuing struggle, and that I sank down and almost fainted. I was aware that Tan Torm was pounding on my back; someone had snatched a tool like a pair of pliers and was forcing the ball down my throat.

At last, thanks to heroic efforts, the refractory bit of paper went down after all, the reviving air entered my lungs. A minute longer, and the Oath would have killed me.

As I gradually regained my senses, I saw the Professor passing out a bright piece of brass, and heard the ringing of the cash register.

"Congratulations, young man!" exclaimed Tan Torm heartily, as he led me away. "The Oath of Fidelity pretty nearly didn't take—but I'm glad you swallowed it after all. Now you're a full-fledged citizen!"

"Oh, am I? And what does that mean?"

"It means you've promised to obey all the laws of the land. It means you've pledged allegiance to Dictator Thuno Flatum, promised to honor him, obey all his orders unquestioningly, and never utter a word against him. It means you've vowed to live a life of one hundred per cent thought-lessness. It means, finally, that you have vowed to live in Wu the rest of your days, and promise never to attempt to leave under penalty of death."

"But I didn't promise anything of the kind!"

"Indeed you did! Didn't you sign the Oath?"

"But I didn't understand what it said."

"That doesn't matter. No one is supposed to understand. Understanding is a sign of thought, and thought is a sign of disloyalty. But you did swallow the Oath, didn't you? That's what makes it legal!"

Now that I had taken the Oath and become a full-fledged citizen, I was permitted to wander unescorted through many of the streets and side-galleries; yet it seemed to me that I had really less freedom than when confined in the Professor's home. I was now officially on the Government books being known as Citizen #44,667,023 XZ, Third Class. I had had my photograph taken and filed with the War Department, my physical measurements recorded and filed with the Police Department, and my toeprints registered and filed with both the War and Police Departments. I was now to receive an official caller.

This event occurred on the fifth "wake" after I had swallowed the Oath. I had been practicing the native writing under the tutorship of Loa; and having noticed a light of warning fondness in her salmon eyes, I was pondering some tactful way of escape when I was startled by the entrance of Moa, who informed me that a visitor wished to see me.

In the next room, a wizened little chalk-face with the features of a fox arose to receive me. "Citizen number 44,667,023 XZ, Third Class?"

"I believe that is my name," said I, although I could never remember whether I was an "XZ" or an "XY."

"I have been detailed to investigate your case," he declared. "As a sub-agent of the Ministry of Public Unemployment, I do not know why the Government has overlooked you so long. I understand, sir, that you have been illegally living in a state of unemployment."

"Illegally—living in a state of unemployment?"

"So I am told! Do you not realize, sir, that unemployment is a crime? That is to say, in all except First Class citizens, who—in order not to take work from the needy—are paid a salary by the State for being unemployed."

Fearing that I was about to be punished for my unwitting offense, I remained silent.

"However, we do not wish to be severe with you," he conceded, still scowling. "This is, after all, your first dereliction, and I have been instructed to let you off with a reprimand. But we must immediately end your unemployment."

"Very well," I assented.

"What valuable labor can you perform?" asked the chalkface, taking a chart out of his pocket and withdrawing across the room so as to read through an instrument that looked like a pair of opera glasses. "Fortunately, owing to the unusual turnover of the present war, an exceptional number of positions are vacant just now."

"Good! What are they?"

"Well, let's see. There are so many it's hard to know where to begin. Now here's one that might do. In the thought-inoculation department of the army."

"Thought-inoculation?"

"Yes; it's necessary to be sure that no private in the army should ever have a thought; otherwise, how could we maintain discipline? It isn't safe to rely on laws only, so we have an anti-thought serum, which acts on the nervous system so as to paralyze the thought centers of the brain. The recruit then has no power left except to obey orders—which makes him an ideal soldier."

"A very good idea," I acknowledged.

"A derivative of the same drug, known as the 'Muffler,' is fed by big business firms to employees. However, a job in this department is not for you!" concluded the agent sadly. "You're a barbarian, and what do barbarians know of thought prevention?"

"More than you think!" I snapped.

"Now here's another good job," he went on, still gazing at the chart by means of the opera glasses. "We're in need of spies. The recent turnover in that department . . ."

"No, thanks! That's really out of my line!"

"But think of the honor! No profession is more esteemed! If you survive, you'll be given a high position in the diplomatic corps. And if, on the other hand, you are turned . . ."

"I'm not covetous about being turned over!"

"It's a glorious death—I mean to say, a glorious turnover! However, if you haven't any push or ambition, I suppose we can find you some humbler job. What about a position in the Mufflar Works?"

"But is that safe?"

"Safe?" The Unemployment Agent glared at me furiously. "Who cares if it's safe? Of course it isn't! Is anything safe in modern life? It's all a matter of the degree of risk! And besides, the salary is high."

"I'm not hankering for a high salary."

"Oh, well, if you're *that* impractical, of course we can fix you up! There's never much demand for low-paying jobs."

Again he stared at the chart, and, after a moment of indecision, suggested, "Let's see now—we might make you valet to a First Class citizen. The wages are not very good, but the work is easy. All you would have to do would be to dust off your master's eye-tubes, or hold his megaphone to his mouth when he speaks. You might adjust his breathing tubes when they get out of order, or arrange his mirrors, or merely stand in his reception hall and look stiff and official when he receives visitors. And whenever he kicks or cuffs you, or calls you names, you would have to bow respectfully and say, 'Thank you, sir!' What do you say?"

"Haven't you anything else?" I asked, in desperation.

The agent scowled again. "You're a hard man to suit! I really don't know what else to offer you. We might place you in the Department of Public Unenlightenment, whose business it is to keep the public from knowing too much. But no! Third Class Citizens are not eligible!"

Once more, he paused, his long black-draped fingers tapping at his knees. At last, with a shout of triumph, he exclaimed, "Ah! now I have it! The very job for you! I congratulate you, young man! You're a lucky individual! A very lucky individual!"

"How so?"

"We need more office help for the Ventilation Company. Too many of its employees have volunteered for the war— and have been turned over. So they have a job just waiting for you in the air-supply division. You begin tomorrow."

"What is the Ventilation Company? And what's the air-supply division?"

"Take my word, it's just the thing for you! No ability required! No thought necessary! Merely do what you're told! And get paid regularly every five wakes!"

"But what's the job like?"

"You'll find out after you're on it! Time enough to worry then!"

Immediately upon hearing my assent, the visitor let out a

whoop of joy; then, drawing forth a printed sheet and a pencil, he flung them at me, and directed, "There! Sign on the barred line!"

Hesitantly I did as directed, and the agent thereupon snatched up the paper, folded it into an inner pocket, instructed me where and when to report for work, bowed, and gingerly left. Not until later did I learn that, as a commission for securing me the work, I had signed over to him all my wages for the first fifty-two wakes.

8. LOA

The Ventilation Company, as I soon discovered, was the most powerful corporation in Wu. It was literally the breath of the country; for it controlled the fresh-air supply. Owned by a group of First Class Citizens, the Company was declared to number Thuno Flatum himself among its stockholders. It was common gossip that more than one war had been commenced on the decision of the Ventiliation officials, and that the current conflict with Zu had been stimulated by them, owing to the fact that the workers had been threatening a strike.

Whatever I might think of the management, I could easily understand the influence of the Company. The more I observed the vast system of air-tubes and wheels, the more I admired the ingenuity of its creators. I was informed how ventilating pipes, opening in narrow ducts in the Overworld, received a constant supply of the fresh air that always blew in that uninhabitable domain; and I was told how the air, forced downward by mighty pumps, mulflar-powered, was delivered in pipes and conduits to every gallery, chamber, and private residence in Wu. This it was that kept the air always fresh and sweet, and averted those noisome odors usually found in underground passageways.

My work for the company began humbly enough. Perched on a stone chair behind a stone railing in a large draughty gallery, where a perfect torrent of air was blowing in order to display "ventilating efficiency," I had to interview customers, hear their complaints, accept the service fees which they paid every twenty wakes, and attempt to sell the various air-machines displayed about the room.

"Do your cleaning by air"; "Have you tried our automatic air-baths?"; "Air-heating engines—guaranteed for hot air"; "Remove dust and germs; air-filters at reduced rates"; "Airrays for health—are you sure your children are getting a sufficiency of A, B, and D?"—these were but a few of the signs that I saw scattered about me on a multitude of curious-looking instruments. Some reminded me of electric toasters, others of vacuum cleaners, and a few were like great dynamos.

Although I still did not know the principles behind these inventions, I was able to sell them easily enough. All I had to do was to look knowing, point to the company's guaranty, and state that the objects were on sale for a limited period only. Prospective customers, particularly if of the gentler or "whiter" sex, were rarely able to resist the lure, even though they understood nothing of the point or purpose of the apparatus they purchased. The sales of articles under such conditions was known as "flumflim," as a result of which, nine tenths of the population was constantly in debt to the Ventilation Company.

The other phases of my work were less interesting. I particularly disliked listening to complaints—and what a stream of them there were! Sometimes the line of complainers reached all the way across the office and fifty yards down the adjoining gallery! Here, for example, would come a testy-looking old chalk-face, with a squeaky wail, "My air-service has been very poor of late! Haven't been able to breathe properly for wakes!" . . .

And after I had promised to send the air-man around to his home to see if his valves were out of order, a querulous young woman, hideous with wrinkles, would exclaim, "See here, young man! Look at this bill! It's plain robbery! The meter must be wrong! We simply couldn't have used that much air!" . . .

Following her in line would be a miserable-looking old woman, who would gloomily display a printed notice, *If you do not pay your bill within five wakes, we will turn off your air supply*. . . . "If you do that, we'll all smother!" she would moan. "You must give us more time to pay!"

But I would have to inform her that the rules of the company made no exception.

There were other complaints—complaints from persons whose air supply was too hot; persons whose air supply was too cold; persons whose air supply had been interrupted; persons with an over-supply of air; persons who had ordered Grade X air for the children and received only Grade Y. You would have supposed the entire country to be suffering from air trouble.

My hours in the Ventilating Office were ten each wake, with one wake out of every five off duty. I was expected to stay half an hour after the office formally closed, in order to clean a great ventilating duct which opened in a corner of the room. I would be obliged to creep into the tube— which was wide enough to admit two men standing abreast —and reach into its dark recesses with a mop, so as to remove all dust and foreign matter. The tube, I was told, connected with the upper Ventilating Corridors, and had to be kept in condition if our product were to remain pure.

After I had been in the Ventilating Office for twenty or thirty wakes, the monotonous routine of my labors was beginning to lull me into the thoughtlessness which was the ideal of the chalk-faces. I had, in fact, been commended for speaking in that automatic manner, and acting with that vacuity of expression, which betokens an empty mind and an efficient worker; hence I began to fear that I would suffer from softening of the brain if I did not find some way to escape. But was escape possible?

Discontent with my work, however, was not the only thing urging me to flee. Although now supposedly a wage-earning citizen, I was still living upon the bounty of Professor Tan Torm, since my pay was going to the Unemployment Agent. Even after he had received his share, I should have to pay an Employment Tax to the Government, and a fee for joining the Ventilation Union. After that, I would have to buy war bonds and pay Peace Taxes, Residence Taxes, Food Taxes, Water Taxes, Air Taxes, etc., all of which were imposed in direct ratio to a man's inability to pay. During the first two and a half years, the more I worked the more deeply I would be in debt.

Now all this would have occasioned me to worry; the natives of Wu consider it a sign of prosperity to be in debt. Besides, Professor Tan Torm, thanks to the profits from his Mulflar stocks, was well able to support me. But what I could not endure was the necessity of living in daily contact with Loa.

I do not blame the poor girl; for some reason—perhaps not unconnected with the fact that most of the eligible males of her own race had been turned over in the current war—she had succumbed to my attractions. Unfortunately, it had never occurred to her that she was not equally attractive, even though she devoted herself for hours a day to her wrinkling machine, diligently putting new wrinkles into her face, since the old ones did not suffice to win my affection! Then she turned, still hopeful, to a new method, and began adding on flesh by "producing powders," "producing baths," a "producing diet," and other means recommended by the dictators of fashion, or "producticians."

Now whatever I might have said about Loa's face when I first met her, I had thought her form perfect. Had she but retained her natural form and unwrinkled countenance, I might have become fond of her! But, as it was, she daily grew more hideous in my eyes. And no word or hint of mine could deter her. Fatness, next to wrinkles, was considered the supreme sign of beauty in women.

Of course, since I had no choice but to remain in the same house with her, I had to be civil; but I thought it the best policy to avoid her as much as possible. Unhappily, I couldn't have done worse. This became evident one day when Professor Tan Torm, pausing in his researches into some dead and buried language, summoned me to his study with an air of importance.

I noticed, as he motioned me to a seat opposite him, that he seemed actually embarrassed.

"My dear young man," he at last confided, rising and coming over to place a fatherly hand on my shoulder, "I have been requested—eh—requested to speak to you by my daughter Loa. For a long time I have been—eh—observing how matters are between you two."

"Why, I—I have always treated her like a gentleman," it was on my lips to say. "I have been observing—yes, observing how matters are between you," he repeated, warming to his subject. "With becoming modesty, you have not made any undue approach. You have kept your feelings to yourself, as was only proper, in view of your Third Class status. You would not insult a Second Class lady by openly declaring yourself. But I have been observing, my dear young man; I have been observing!"

Throughout this speech, I sat gaping at the Professor wide-eyed and with loose-hanging jaws.

"Yes, I have been observing!" he went on. "I have been consulting with Loa, as is only a father's place, and have been assured that she—she reciprocates your feelings."

"Reciprocates—my feelings?"

"Yes. It is only natural, young man, that you should be overwhelmed—it isn't every day that a Second Class lady will look at a Third Class suitor. But I have no prejudices in the matter at all, my boy. We're all human, when you come to think of it, even if we can't all be considered equal. Besides, though you're a barbarian by birth, you've recently grown civilized. So, my daughter being willing, I can only give my blessings. May your union be crowned with—"

But I did not hear the end of the sentence. In an agony of protest, I shot out of my seat so suddenly that my head collided with the projecting steel frame of the Professor's thesaurus, which I had not noticed in my agitation.

When I came to myself, Loa was bending over me tenderly, tears in her eyes, a bottle of some strong-smelling solution in her hands. And in the background I saw the Professor looming, still smiling the same benignant smile. "Poor young man!" I thought I heard him say. "The shock of this happiness was more than he could bear!"

It was then that I decided upon flight.

9. FLIGHT

It was what was known to the chalk-faces as the "mid-sleep." The lights of the public galleries had been dimmed; the lamps of the houses had been extinguished; the ventilating currents turned low. Only an occasional belated wayfarer or military guard, darting through the deserted thoroughfares on his little scoot, gave proof that life still went on in the land of Wu.

At this silent hour, when the house doors stared in black, almost invisible lines along the empty passageways, you might have seen a figure stealthily emerging from one of the doors, and slinking off down a narrow side-corridor.

Only half a dozen hours had passed since Professor Tan Torm had made his revelation; and I was now resigned to taking whatever risks lay in the outside world. My preparations, it is true, had been less complete than I could have desired; but I had found time to ransack the Professor's pantry, and to secrete a pound or two of concentrated food in my clothing, in addition to a flask of water. As for my direction —I must confess that I was none too certain of it, but I had found an old map in the kitchen closet and had studied it as well as my haste permitted.

Do not suppose that I had not weighed the dangers. I knew that I might be punished as a vagrant or a spy; I might be charged with "disgorging" my Oath of Fidelity, and become subject to the death penalty. But I had knowingly placed these penalties in the scale beside the certainty that, if I remained in Tan Torm's home, I should have to marry his daughter.

For several hours I advanced with the caution of a cat, and almost with the silence of a cat, since I had removed my heavy native sandals. But I was not certain what to do after the sleep was over. Suddenly I was aware of an ear-ripping sound, like a siren blast; the lights in the galleries flashed into brilliance, and I realized that a new wake had begun.

I was now in a section I had never before visited. The narrowness and dinginess of the galleries; the dusty, dirt-encrusted walls and floors; the foulness of the air, which was not clear and filtered as in other regions; the unsavory odors; the naked glare of the lights, unprotected by the yellow-green screens common everywhere else—these showed that I was in an inferior district.

This fact became even more evident when, after a time, little round holes in the ground began to discharge swarms of people into all the passageways. Never before had I seen such desolate-looking chalk-faces. The majority were in rags; some of the men were without even the skirts that betokened masculinity. As for the women—they were equally tattered, but they had the advantage of being less fat and wrinkled than their more prosperous sisters, and I thought many of them quite attractive.

Was this a district of criminals and outcasts? But no! A prominent sign informed me that this was a "Residential section, Third Class." Now I understood why the Third Class was called the Hungry Class.

With these poor wretches I shared the concentrated food I had taken from the Professor's house—and it was pathetic to see how eagerly they snatched at the morsels.

"What's the matter?" I asked one of the beggars, as I doled out my last mite. "Don't any of you needy folk work?"

"Don't any of us work?" the man stared at me with hostility and surprise. "What a question! Say, you must be one of those Second Class swells."

I assured him that, on the contrary, I was Third Class, but from another part of the country. At this, he looked a little mollified. "Well, I don't know how it is where you come from, but here we all work. We have to, on account of the unemployment law. Even the children—those not in the army—work from seven years of age. But we don't get any wages till the First Class citizens take out their dividends, guaranteed by law at fifty per cent a year. What is left is just about enough to pay the landlords, whose returns are also guaranteed on a percentage basis."

"But aren't there any laws protecting you?"

"Protecting us? That would be Government interference in private affairs."

Indignant, I proceeded on my way; finally, after several hours, I found myself in a more pleasant and airier section, though one not wholly to my liking. The caverns were much roomier, but the atmosphere was vaguely disagreeable with the odor of smoke.

I approached an open space, where acres of huge cardboard boxes were piled to a height of fifty feet, surrounded by tall barbed-wire fences. But on consulting my map, I was unable to say whether I was in the "Storage Grottoes," "The Surplus Food Chambers," or the "Military Warehouses," all of which looked alike on the chart.

Pressing on my way around the mountains of boxes, I soon discovered the source of the smoke. A few hundred yards ahead of me, the door of an enormous furnace opened.

Two men were working in front of the furnace. Stripped to the waist, grimy with soot and perspiration, they reached for the cardboard boxes, throwing them one after another through the furnace mouth.

Assuming that the boxes contained waste matter or fuel with which to keep the fires burning, I hastened inquiringly forward. And, as I drew near, the men paused to rest from their exertions, while mopping their steamy brows and panting heavily.

"Well," I heard one of them declare after closing the furnace door, "that makes eleven gross so far this wake."

"Nearer twelve, if you're asking me," stated the other. "Say, have we got to those medical supplies yet?"

"Not yet! We're still working on the clothes! There's a couple of hundred tons more to burn, and after that I don't know how many thousands of tons of food capsules."

"Pardon, friends," I said, stepping to within a few feet of them, "being a stranger around these parts, I'm just a little curious as to what's in those boxes."

I was now so close to the men that they could not see me clearly.

"Great caverns! You *must* be a stranger. I thought everyone knew they were filled with food and clothes, and such things!"

"Not good food and clothes?"

The two workers stared at me oddly. "Why not? Aren't we getting rid of the country's overproduction?"

"Haven't you ever been to school?" challenged the second. "Don't you know overproduction is bad for business? It causes depressions, low dividends, and low wages. So when we've made more of a product than anyone can buy, the only thing to do is to burn it. 'Burn your way to prosperity!' —that's an old motto. The more we burn, the more prosperity."

"Why, that's elementary," added the first. "By destroying

things, you raise prices, which is the chief object of civilization. The more you have to pay for things, the more prosperous you will be. A high standard of paying is the first test of progress."

Personally, I have never claimed to know anything of economics, so I humbly asked why the surplus could not be distributed among the Hungry Class.

Even before the words were out of my mouth, I could see the faces of my hearers growing wry with horror. "How can we give the food and clothing to the Hungry Class? They haven't anything to pay for it, have they?"

"Raise your standard of paying them!" I suggested.

"By my father's pink eyes!" gasped the other man. "He's a revolutionist, that's what he is! Radicals like him want to ruin the country! Now get out of here, with your crazy ideas, or I'll report you to the Overhears!"

This argument being a clinching one, particularly when backed up with two heavy pairs of fists, I started away hastily.

10. VICTORY PARADE

Half an hour later, when I was still gradually winding my way upward through the labyrinths, I came out unexpectedly on a broad thoroughfare. Great multitudes of chalk-faces had convened there, lining themselves along the sides of the avenue, but leaving the center clear. I mingled with the crowds, and pushed forward so as to secure a position in the front row. Once more, I was protected by the inability of the natives to see things close at hand.

No sooner had I edged my way to the front than the spectators jumped and stamped in glee, flung their arms high in air, and shouted till their throats were hoarse. Although I made an effort to join in the chorus, it was not quite clear to me what they were shouting about. I thought, however, I could make out something like "Long live the green and vermilion! Long live the green and vermilion!"

At first, the impression came to me that I was about to witness a football game. But as the tumult subsided, a huge banner hanging from the ceiling reminded me that green and vermilion were the national colors of Wu. A portly chalk-face just to my right turned to me genially and remarked, with an expectant smile, "Well, Thuno Flatum be praised! They'll be coming any minute now!"

"S'pose they will," I agreed.

"This is General Bing's greatest triumph," went on my neighbor. "Just imagine, he's retaken three fifths of the upper left-hand corner of Nullnull—at a cost of only a million and a quarter turnovers! Marvelous!"

"Marvelous!" I concurred.

"True, he couldn't hold it very long. He was outnumbered too strongly. But, great caverns! he did keep it a good three quarters of a wake! They say that, when retreating, he didn't have to vacate more than four fifths of the lower left-hand corner of Nullnull, at a cost of another million and a quarter turnovers. An extraordinary strategic victory!"

"Extraordinary!" I acknowledged.

"So it's only proper that our good Thuno Flatum should grant a triumphal procession! Look! Here they come!"

Suddenly the mob let out such a howl that I had to clap my palms to my ears. To the accompaniment of blaring horns, and of a clanging instrument known as a "banger," which made a noise resembling a cannonade, an elegant-looking procession of dignitaries rode into view on slow-moving little scoots. On one of the foremost cars, surrounded by a bodyguard of a hundred warriors and several scores of obsequious valets, rode a man in a gorgeous crimson uniform. His exalted rank would have been apparent from the long ear-tubes, the projecting eye-tubes, the nose-tubes and mouth-tubes, and his dwarfish stature and wizened legs—all of which proved him to be a First Class citizen!

Just why the General should have been so popular with the Second and Third Classes was more than I could understand. But countless eyes shed tears of joy.

"You see, he bears a charmed life," stated my portly neighbor. "All generals bear charmed lives. In order to keep their lives charmed, they direct the battles from strongholds fifty galleries to the rear, for what a loss to the country if they should be—eh—turned over!"

The main body of the procession was now passing—and a gallant sight it was! There were several other generals, who, like Commander-in-Chief Bing, were dressed either in crimson, or in crimson striped with black; there were hundreds of banners of green and vermilion, and several yellow-and-purple banners, said to have been captured during the strategic retreat from Nullnull. There were scores of large scoots laden with blackened uniforms taken from the enemy. There were several dozen war heroes, who had received the Dictatorial Badge of Honor, and were so covered with decorations that it was impossible to see their faces. There were innumerable placards proclaiming the vastness of the recent victories, which, it seemed, were without precedent "in the history of civilized massacre." And there were, finally, thousands of common soldiers, who walked twenty abreast, with the peculiar high-swinging foot motion of the native infantry.

All these men wore helmets, of the peculiar hatchet shape I had already observed; but instead of swords or rifles, they carried long poles. On the top of each of these I observed curious round glittering objects which, at the first glimpse, looked most attractive, for their wiry sheaths caught the light and flashed it back. But on a closer view, I shuddered; under each of the gleaming metal coverings was a skull.

While I reeled backward, I heard the cheers of the throng. "Look at the proofs of our victory! Proofs of our victory! Proofs of our victory! All praise! All praise! All praise!"

Following the foot soldiers, dozens of huge vans came rumbling down the avenue, electrically propelled, and bearing great machines that I can only describe as dragons of a hundred necks, since their steel bodies bristled with scores of long tapering tubes, twenty feet high, and pointing in all directions, like the throats of siege guns.

"Just look at them! Great caverns, just look!" sputtered my neighbor. "The lightning-spitters!"

"Lightning what?"

"Lightning-spitters! Of course, you've heard of them! One of the most remarkable inventions of modern times!"

Even as he spoke, a blade of orange electricity shot from one of the machines, darting to the ceiling in a swift zigzag; and was succeeded instantly by blades of green and crimson, while miniature thunders rolled.

Now I understood; these machines were the source of the lightnings that had wiped out whole armies in the battle cavern.

"Of course, those were only toy lightnings, for exhibition purposes," my neighbor rambled on.

"What's the principle behind them?"

My neighbor shrugged. "How do I know? It's a carefully guarded secret. However, they do say that the power of Mulflar is used to generate electricity in the machine—and generate it in such excess that the engine becomes supercharged, and releases its energy through the tubes in tremendous lightning blades."

"I see," said I. "The machine becomes somewhat like a thundercloud supercharged with positive electricity—"

"Thunder what?"

I realized that I had used the wrong illustration, for, of course, thunderclouds were not known underground.

"The only trouble," proceeded my neighbor, after I had vainly tried to explain the nature of a thundercloud, "is in controlling the lightnings. Of course, the army boasts of its precision aiming, but everyone knows it's only the aiming that's precise, not the actual shooting—you can never tell just where the lightning will strike."

"I should call that a fatal difficulty."

"Yes, fatal is the word. Wherever it hits, it's certain to kill —that is to say"—here my neighbor paused, greatly embarrassed—"that is to say, to turn over some of the enemy. And that, after all, is the only thing that counts."

I was about to reply that I probably owed my life to the nature of the enemy's precision aiming, when all at once the crowd broke into the National Anthem.

Unfortunately, I have forgotten all the stanzas except the first, which I give in a translation that does scant justice to the magnificence of the original, but will illustrate the theme and spirit of the whole:

> Let us fight forever!
>   We'll be conquered never
>   While we've heads to sever
>   From our brutish foes!
> Let us fight forever
>   With a gay endeavor!
>   We are keen and clever
>   With electric blows!

The crowd had just completed the twenty-first stanza, and was singing the chorus with resounding gusto, when I made an observation that instantly ended all my interest in the celebration. Among the throngs across the gallery, I caught sight of an ugly-looking chalk-face, with thin slits of eyes and a twisted nose, who was staring at me with such an intent scrutiny that I felt a chill traveling down my spine.

Now I remembered that I was a fugitive from the law. With a tremor of terror, I pushed my way back into the crowd, resolved on instant flight; the dread of being taken back to face the violet ray or marry Loa lent haste to my footsteps.

11. THE PHONOSCOPE

I can scarcely recall where I wandered in my haste;
I only know that I put on my best sprinting gait as I slipped
around a bend in the corridor and off along a narrow, down-
curving passageway. Later, I passed another turn in the gallery, and came out, to my surprise, among a crowd in a wide
grotto dominated by a sign in glowing crystalline letters:
PHONOSCOPE THEATRE: ADMISSION, ONE BRASS FINGER.

Now I knew that a "brass finger" was a fair-sized sum of
money—equivalent to the returns from an average day's
labor. Needless to say, I had never yet had such a sum; nevertheless, mingling with the crowd, I pressed forward in a
long line filing past a ticket-taker. I had worked out my
strategy, based upon the chalk-faces' inability to see things
near at hand. There was a little strip of cardboard in my
pocket (it had been used for jotting down notes during my
lessons with Loa); I thrust this into the ticket-taker's hand,
and cried, "Free pass!" He would have to hold it off at a
distance, and examine it with binoculars, before he discovered the fraud; meanwhile, I allowed the impatient mob to
press me forward past the theatre door.

It seemed to me that, as I entered, I heard a confused
shouting outside, and some imprecations calling down the
Seven Furies on someone's head. However, I remained nicely
hidden among the crowd as I shuffled down a long aisle in
the most peculiar amusement place I had ever seen.

Beneath a ceiling that arched to a hundred feet or more,
long rows of benches sloped downward toward an open central space or stage, on which a tall chalk-face with a long
three-pointed beard was holding forth sonorously. All spectators, however, were looking and listening through queer
instruments projecting from the benches and rarely seemed
to heed the speaker.

I slipped into one of the seats as quickly and inconspicu-
ously as possible, and began to examine the instruments in
front of me. There were tubes like earphones, attached by
wires to a little electric socket; and there were other tubes

resembling small telescopes, also attached by wires to a socket.

While I was struggling with the tubes, I heard the voice of the speaker:

"Fellow citizens of the Second and Third Class, you are about to witness an extraordinary exhibition. Until three years ago, when that marvelous invention the Phonoscope was perfected, it would not have been possible safely to witness what you are now about to see. For the benefit of those still unacquainted with this masterly machine, I would say that if you will arrange the eye and ear pieces, and step on the little lever to your left, you will be just in time for the beginning of the performance."

In a few seconds more, I had arranged to adjust the earphones and telescope-like tubes; and, following instructions, witnessed a remarkable transformation.

The theatre, the long rows of benches, the tall form of the speaker had vanished from view; the shuffling, grating noises of people passing down the aisles, the sonorous voice of the long-bearded man in front had all been obliterated. But new sounds, new sights crowded upon my senses.

"You now behold the battlefield a hundred miles away," I heard the speaker proclaim, when, in order to relieve my aching ears, I had removed the earphones. "The Phonoscope is connected with scores of points on the battlefield. Motion-picture cameras, at the other end of the line, are constantly photographing the sights, which are conveyed to you by an apparatus like television, except that you may see directly instead of gazing at a screen. At the same time, radio transmitters catch the sounds and bring them to your ears; so that you may see and hear the battle from a safe distance."

I saw the army, with yellow and purple banners afloat, advancing across the field; but I was so interested in the speaker's words that I was reluctant to clap on the earphones again.

"Thanks to the Phonoscope," he went on, "war has become much more interesting than ever before. Previously we had only the newspapers, altogether too tame. Or else we had to go to war ourselves—in which case we were all too likely to be—er—turned over. But now, for a mere Brass Finger, we can enjoy the spectacle without enduring any of its hardships."

At this point, my attention was distracted from the

speaker to the battlefield. Out of little round orifices on the cavern walls, showers of phosphorescent silvery orbs had flashed, falling like shooting stars upon the floor where the purple-and-yellow army was maneuvering. And all at once those regular, serried ranks became like a column of ants deluged with hot water. The wildest disorder prevailed; squadrons of men seemed literally to wither away, while other myriads fled in all directions.

All at once, the announcer broke in. "Look carefully, my friends! Look carefully! The Subterrain is coming! The Subterrain! The Subterrain!"

Anxious not to miss anything, I clapped the earphones on again, and glanced once more at the battlefield. And, as I did so, a scene of shattering fury burst upon my view.

For one instant, I was aware of the wide cavern floor, but the next instant, all this had vanished. There was a terrific upheaval of earth and rock, which for a fraction of a second covered all things in a great blur; the walls of the cavern sagged, and in places collapsed in avalanches. The floor became jagged as a lunar landscape, with sharp craters and deep ravines, and hillocks, bluffs and gulches where all had been flat and smooth a moment before. And in my ears was such a thundering that I reeled and was all but knocked over.

Hastily snatching off the earphones, I remained gazing with absorbed interest upon that scene. I could no longer see any trace of the purple-and-yellow army. The fugitives, no less than the victims, had all disappeared. And as the visible sign of their destruction, a long, thin, dark metallic tube was projecting from the broken center of the floor, like the neck of some great carniverous dinosaur.

"Ah, that is fine, isn't it, my friends? A most satisfactory enemy turnover! Most satisfactory! You see that long tube jutting above the floor? That is the tip of the Subterrain! No other contrivance has produced half so great a turnover. It was the creation of the renowned engineer Hyz Cre. Why not make a machine, he asked, which would travel underground as our submersible vessels travel beneath rivers and lakes?

"The result was the Subterrain. The principles behind it are admirably simple; the weapon, which is a relatively slender steel cylinder accommodating five or six men, gradually works its way through a narrow excavation already prepared for it by a machine like a powerful well-borer—the 'cave blaster,' which operates by the power of Mulflar and has made it possible to dig our gigantic war galleries.

"But let me tell about the Subterrain itself. Affixed to its prow is an electric dredge, which tears up the earth before it and deposits it behind; by this means, the Subterrain digs its way forward at the rate of a quarter of a mile an hour. Meanwhile its crew, confined in their narrow compartment, are kept alive by air supplied through long connecting tubes, in the manner of divers. A delicate instrument, with a radio attachment, informs the men when they are in the neighborhood of an enemy cavern—for, of course, the machine is never used except in wartime. Being within a few feet of a hostile gallery, the Subterrain halts, retreats a short distance into the tunnel it has bored and launches a Mulflar torpedo —whose effects, as you have observed, are highly gratifying.

"Great as are the merits of the Subterrain," the speaker continued, "it cannot be denied that it has some minor drawbacks. One of these is that there is no longer any security for the civilian population during wartime. You never know when a Subterrain, boring unnoticed beneath your feet, may launch a Mulflar bomb directly at you. It is impossible to say how many thousands of noncombatants have been turned over in this manner since the war began. Even First Class citizens have not been spared—an intolerable form of barbarity which will now be ended by a humanitarian treaty which has just been negotiated, confining attacks of the Subterrain to regions occupied by Second and Third Class citizens."

It was at this point that I lost interest in the speech. I had risen to leave, when my eyes were riveted on a chalk-face just appearing at the door. There at the entrance, staring at me with a fascinated gaze, was my friend of the slit eyes and twisted nose!

Not tempted to make his closer acquaintance, I darted toward a dark passageway marked *Exit*. And instantly he set up such a howl that the whole theatre was aroused, and the speaker, startled, halted midway in his address. "Thief! Robber! Bandit!" scores of shouts dinned from behind me. "Catch him! Catch him! He's a deserter! Grab him! Turn him over!"

As I darted into the passageway at a speed that did justice to my college track training, it was only too evident that the slit-eyed detective had mistaken me for someone else. But I did not wait to argue about his error. I dashed away with half the theatre audience at my heels.

As I rushed around the bends of the branching corridors, I could feel the blood-lusting of the rabble behind me, could hear their cries growing more excited, could hear the rattling of pebbles and rocks hurled at me by the onsweeping patriots.

Then suddenly, above the din and screaming of the throng, my ears caught the screech of a whistle, and I knew that the police were being summoned. In that critical moment, while my breath came hard and fast and my heart hammered like a great weight, I slipped around a turn that hid me temporarily from my pursuers. And, at the same instant, the saving suggestion came to me. There, on the pavement before me, was an iron lid as large as the manhole of a sewer, its top bearing the prominent letters, PROPERTY OF THE VENTILATION COMPANY! KEEP OFF!

Instantly, I thrust the iron lid out of place. With a leap and a plunge, I dropped into the gaping black hole; and with a furious wrench of my arms, as I came to halt on the slippery steel surface, I pulled the lid into place above me.

The next second, secure in that cranny amid the darkness, I could hear the mob surging and stamping above my head.

12. COMPANY HERO

It is impossible to say just how long I lay there in the gloom. It may have been only minutes, but it seemed hours, while the howls of the rabble came to my ears through the thin slit of iron just above.

I felt an intense desire to creep farther down into my hiding place. But my feet were resting on a ledge only a foot or two wide, and vacancy seemed to yawn beneath. I felt sure that I was on the brink of a precipice, for a pebble or fragment of metal, accidentally dislodged by my foot, rattled for a long while as it descended. Meantime I was in as uncomfortable a position as you could imagine: huddled against the iron while a chilly breath of air blew continually over me. I was not only catching cold, but—much worse!—had reason to fear that I might sneeze.

At last, however, the tumult of the multitude subsided, and I could hear the shouting at a distance, until gradually it died out entirely.

Even so, it did not seem safe to lift the iron lid—might some member of the mob not be lurking near? And so I remained crouched there in the darkness, waiting, waiting.

But after a while, I again heard the sound of voices—voices lifted in loud excitement. "The ventilation! What's happened to the ventilation?"

"Looks to me like the work of those spies from Zu!"

"Disturbance seems to center somewhere up this way," grumbled a third. "Those blazing complaints are coming in for miles around!"

"By my mother's white skin!" resumed the first. "If anything got into one of those pipes, it would automatically stop the air over the whole district!"

As I listened to this conversation, a thrill of horror and a sense of guilt shot over me.

"Remember that last time," continued one of the men. "When those big rats got caught in one of the tubes? We had to shoot in some Mulflar and blow them to cinders!"

By this time the men were almost directly above me, and I was overwhelmed by the desire to sneeze. The best I could

68

do was to muffle it, so that it had a stifled but unfortunately all-too-loud sound not in the least like a sneeze. I could hear the men pausing above my head. "Great caverns! What's that?" one of them snapped. "Didn't it sound like a rat?"

"If it's one rat, it's a whole colony! They grow big down here, you know."

"Well, here's the very place," took up the first. "Right in this air-tube! We'll fix them, all right! And I could hear the man rattling the iron lid above my head.

Never before had I wished so ardently for the power of invisibility. I resorted to the desperate expedient of hanging over the brim, holding onto the ledge with both hands, while my body lay along an iron surface sloping at an angle of forty-five degrees.

No sooner had I gained this position than I heard the lid clanging out of place; and a flood of light burst upon me. In the glare above, several chalk-faces were staring down at me. "There it is! The biggest I ever saw!"

"Well, we'll get rid of him fast enough!" the second man declared. "Just one minute there! Let's have that brush! And here—the poison spray!"

It had never occurred to me, until that moment, to have any sympathy for a trapped rat. But I could feel boundless sympathy as a huge brush, malodorous with some vile-smelling concoction, was thrust through the opening directly at my face.

I do not know whether I cried out in my terror. But I do know that my hands, as I struggled to evade that oncoming weapon, lost their precarious grip on the ledge. The next instant, I had gone shooting off into the darkness.

Each man at sometime in his life, I suppose, experiences things that seem miraculous. But for me no miracle ever surpassed my survival from that plunge. I could easily have broken my head or caved in my ribs against the steel projections of the ventilating system. Nothing but chance, and the fact that the ventilating tubes were not perpendicular, saved me from a sudden and horrible turnover. Down, down, down I shot, skimming around curves, banging against bends and corners, tumbling head over heels in a mad dash wherein it was impossible to regain my balance. Only now and then could I momentarily check my speed, when the tube, for a few feet, became almost horizontal; but always it would dip sharply again, and I would go falling once more.

It seemed that I had traveled for miles when suddenly I

collided with a wall and came to a halt, stunned and bruised. With difficulty, I picked myself up, while noting with relief a slit of light through the partition I had just struck. It was, in fact, not a wall, but a partly open door.

Then, as my dazed senses gradually cleared, I became aware of something familiar in my surroundings. Did this not resemble the ventilating duct which opened on the office where I had worked? Still feeling somewhat dizzy, I crept through the doorway, and found myself in a large, well-lighted chamber—not, indeed, my former place of employment, but so similar that I knew it to be another office of the Ventilating Company.

Before I had had time to reflect upon my plight, or wonder what to do, I was startled to see four or five men rushing out of several adjoining rooms.

Upon seeing me, they stopped short, with loud, excited cries. Had I had the energy, I would have crawled back into the ventilating tube. But I was so weak that I could only drop to the floor.

"Who in the sacred name of Wu may you be? Where did you come from?" demanded the foremost. "Don't you know it's forbidden to trespass on the ventilating ducts?"

"Of course I know!" I moaned. And then, as a last resource, "But I—I'm also an employee of the company."

"Oh, you're an employee of the company?" The chalk-faces stared at one another significantly, and their manner became slightly more friendly. "Well, we'd better go and report to the manager!"

With my last remaining gasp of energy, I sought to dissuade them. But, plead as I might, the ventilation men were inexorable. "No, we must report to the manager! The rules require it!"

This assertion was the last straw; merciful unconsciousness swept over me.

I remained unconscious for a long while—so I was afterwards told. When I came to myself again, I was lying on a sort of bed or couch, with a sheet drawn up to my neck; all my clothes had been removed, except for a single shirtlike covering, and my head was swathed in bandages. To my right rose a bare wall, and above me, at a height of three or four feet, stared a blank ceiling. To the left, across an aisle little more than a yard wide, were neat rows of berths, arranged one above the other three tiers high. Dozens of men reclined there, one to each cot, all of them buried up to the neck beneath the sheets.

I saw wires, with pulley-like attachments, which ran through minute holes in the ceiling to each of the berths, and which carried little rattling cars no larger than a small ink bottle. I saw vials and tubes, filled with variously colored liquids and powders, which stood on a neatly numbered shelf just above my head; and I noted that a copper wire, attached to my left wrist, ran the length of the bed and out through an opening in the wall, while similar wires led to each of the other berths.

But I was too weary to wonder; I sank back upon a pillow composed of some strawlike substance, closed my eyes, and fell into a refreshing slumber. . . .

From this sleep I was aroused with a start by the sound of someone talking; it took me a minute to discover that the voice, transmitted by radio, issued from the ceiling behind me.

Unfortunately, I had missed the first words, but, judging from what I later heard, I believe I can reproduce the whole fairly accurately:

"Mechanical Hospital Number 807 QL, Third Class! It is now precisely fifteen minutes and eleven seconds after the start of the wake! Time to take your morning tonic! This you will find on the shelf above you, Number 36 A, in the blue vial. Dissolve two pellets in the distilled water which you will find in Number 36 B. Drink slowly, and finish with an ounce of the liquid in 36 C. Then recline, and return to sleep. Our next announcement will be for the midmorning repast!"

With uncanny suddenness, the machine snapped into silence. The occupants of all the other berths, rising slightly out of bed, reached for the indicated vials and consumed the contents as the voice had directed. For my own part, however, I merely sank down into bed again.

A moment later, irritated by the wire about my wrist, which dug into the flesh and checked the circulation, I pulled at the obstruction viciously and succeeded in removing it. But no sooner had I accomplished this than I was shocked to hear a bell clanging just above my head. And, from the radio-speaker on the ceiling, a voice bawled reprovingly:

"The patient who has just removed his wrist register will kindly fasten it on again. We cannot expect to cure him unless this is left securely in place. For the benefit of any persons still ignorant of the facts, we may repeat that the wrist register is the essence of modern medicine. By means of a faint but constant electric current, it records the patient's pulse, temperature, and respiration, which are noted down in the chartroom by automatic wired connections. Thus we are aware of the patient's condition minute by minute, and are able to do without expensive attendants. It is this device which has made the Mechanical Hospital possible, and has enabled Third Class citizens to enjoy the benefits of modern medical knowledge."

I hastily readjusted the wire.

Let me now pass over the space of a few hours, during which I dozed from time to time, and from time to time took food or drugs in accordance with the radio instructions, which were constantly awakening me from the most invigorating sleep. The most important event occurred toward the close of the wake, when the radio announced "Visitors' Hour."

Needless to say, this announcement did not interest me, for who was there to see me?

But no sooner had Visitors' Hour begun than I heard four or five pairs of feet shuffling down the aisle in my direction; and was electrified at the sight of several familiar faces. These were the employees of the Ventilation Company who had threatened to call the manager. Among them —might heaven preserve me!—I noticed the tigerish face of the manager himself!

Only on one other occasion—when I had begun work in the Ventilation Office—had I encountered this personage, who answered to the name of Go Gral. But never could I forget that occasion, or drive his bullish, square-jawed face from my mind; I thought of him somewhat as the small boy thinks of the rod-wielding pedagogue. I closed my eyes.

"There he is!" exclaimed one of the visitors. "All beaten up from knocking about inside the tube!"

"No wonder!" declared a second. "He must have gone through two miles of pipe!"

"When did you say he would be well again?" I heard the voice of the manager. "Naturally, we can do nothing until then!"

"They say he'll be out in a few wakes. Only suffering from shock, along with surface cuts and bruises."

"Good! It would be awkward if he had been turned over."

"It was a wonderful performance," one of the ventilating employees was declaring. "By the lowest caverns, I never saw anything like it. To creep for miles through the ventilation tubes, all the way from his office to ours! To dust them out and brush away all obstructions, at the risk of his life! I assure you, Go Gral, we were all dumbfounded! The best of it was that he succeeded! From the moment he left the duct, the air currents were working properly again!"

"Such modesty I never saw before!" a second employee was relating. "Can you believe it, Go Gral, when we promised to report the affair to you, he tried to dissuade us! He seemed positively eager not to take the credit!"

"Such self-effacement," rumbled the manager, as I opened my eyes, "is the ideal that the company demands! We will not forget such devoted service!"

And then, nodding to me with a smile while I vainly strove to get in a word, "Quiet there, my good man, quiet! You need all your energy to get well. But I want you to know that you will be rewarded, my dear man, you will be rewarded. And now, goodbye! Goodbye!"

"Goodbye! Goodbye!" echoed the other ventilation employees; and all bowed low.

As they filed off down the aisle, I could hear the manager's pleased voice: "We will report this exploit in our monthly booklet, as an example to all our workers!"

While I was wondering if they were crazy or I, I heard heavy footsteps thumping toward me along the aisle, and glanced out of bed to receive a new shock. Waddling forward as fast as her obese form would permit, and with an ingratiating smile on her wrinkled face, was none other than Loa! And behind her, benignantly beaming, loomed Professor Tan Torm.

"Well, well, well, my boy," rattled the latter, as he made his way toward my berth. "Here you are at last! We've been waiting for you in the reception room a full hour—a full hour, by my watch! They're not very courteous in these Third Class hospitals. But Loa wanted to come—so here we are! It would hardly be proper to let a respectable girl come alone to such quarters."

"Oh, my dear, my dear, I'm so glad we've found you!" exclaimed Loa. "We've heard all about it! The *Wakely Screamer* tells the story in headlines! It even has pictures showing how you climbed up the ventilation tube! How brave you were, my dear! Oh, how brave! It makes me feel honored to know—well, to know I can call such a man my very own!" And she held out her capacious arms as if to enfold me.

"You can't imagine how nervous I was about you last night, my dear, when you didn't come home!" continued Loa. "I was afraid you were lost! But Father—Father wasn't worried. He was so absorbed in his researches into the antiquity of the hyphen, he only growled and said what if you did get lost? The streets are as safe as our own home! But I didn't get a wink of sleep—not one wink!—until I read the news in the *Screamer*!"

No defeated general, suddenly realizing that his most carefully laid strategy has failed, could have had a more sinking sensation than I felt at that moment.

"My dear boy," the Professor continued, glancing disparagingly about the room, "what a miserable rathole they've given you to sleep in! You can't remain here! We'll arrange to take you home immediately!"

"Yes," agreed Loa, beaming upon me. "You poor dear! I'll take care of you myself!"

Overwhelmed at this idea, I opened my mouth to protest; but the words stuck in my throat. Instead, I uttered something halfway between a gasp and a sob.

"No, no, dear, don't exert yourself!" Loa urged. "Don't thank us yet! You're still too weak to speak! But we'll see the authorities and have all arrangements made."

The truth is that I *was* too weak to speak—much too weak. As Professor Tan Torm nodded goodbye and disappeared down the aisle, followed by his daughter, I relapsed into a coma.

It is doubtful if I could have recuperated at all had it not been for a message that came to me an hour or two later, sealed in an envelope that shot to my bedwise through a pneumatic tube. This helped me more than all the hospital tonics, and enabled me, for a time, to drive out the dread vision of Loa.

The letter, written on the embossed stationery of the Ventilation Company, ran as follows:

#44,667,023 XZ, Third Class
c/o Mechanical Hospital #807 QL, Third Class.
Dear Sir:

By virtue of your distinguished services on the line of duty, we are honored, on the recommendation of our

Manager, Go Gral, to promote you from Ventilating Clerk to Ventilating Inspector, the appointment to take effect as soon as you are able to return to work. In your new capacity, your hours will be half what you formerly served, and by way of compensation, your salary will be doubled. We remain

Appreciatively yours,

THE VENTILATION COMPANY OF WU

(Per Do Quel, Eleventh Vice-President)

13. THE EXAMINATION

For seven wakes I remained in the hospital. Even though I disliked the place, still I lived in hourly dread of being sent back to Professor Tan Torm's home. I knew that he had applied to have me taken out; but what I did not know was that a thousand formalities had to be observed while the application was processed. In the course of time, indeed, Tan Torm's application was duly approved—but not until three wakes after my discharge.

It is a testimony to a naturally strong constitution that I was able to escape in one week; the newspaper reporters alone were enough to give me a daily attack of chills and fever. The gentlemen of the press, thanks to the special privileges of their profession, would descend upon me at any time of the day or night, in order to secure my personal story for the *Wakely Blare*, or in order to learn my views on the topics of the day—such as the reasons for the peculiar charms of the women of Wu, or the desirability of improving men's styles by further enlarging the V-slit on the back.

Naturally, I refused to reply, for I did not see how my work for the Ventilation Company qualified me to express myself on native fashions, feminine beauty, or politics. The reporters, however, seemed to feel otherwise; I was later shown long articles in which I was described as "speaking volubly," and read the views credited to me on subjects so diverse as the genius of Thuno Flatum, the natural superiority of Wu to Zu, the future of the scoot, and (I quote) "Why I Am in Love with Wrinkles."

It was with intense misgivings that I awaited my release, for how could I avoid returning to Tan Torm's home? Luckily, this problem was solved for me by the Ventilation Company. Upon presenting myself for work, I was informed that they provided living quarters for their inspectors in a great dormitory, so that they might be subject to call at any hour. While it was not compulsory to reside there, I had no hesitation; hastily I dictated a letter to Tan Torm and his daughter, thanking them for past favors, regretting I could no longer accept their hospitality, and assuring them I would not forget to repay the sum I had borrowed.

As was to be expected, in view of my doubled salary, my new labors were much less exacting than the old. It was my daily duty to travel from place to place, inspecting the ventilating tubes and outlets, and reporting obstructions; and in order to accomplish this task, wherein I was pretty much my own master, I had to ride one of the company-owned scoots; however, I found it easy enough to run the machine, whose driving mechanism—guaranteed as "moron-proof,"—was as simple as that of an elevator. But I was never able to balance myself on it cross-legged with the native ease. And since there were no traffic rules, survival was a matter of sheer luck.

By taking roundabout ways, and choosing the less-frequented thoroughfares, I succeeded in reducing the risk; in the first few months, I only suffered minor mishaps. Except for some bruises on the head and shoulders, and abraded knee and a sprained wrist, I might be said to have escaped unscathed.

In the course of my new activities, I had an opportunity to inspect the ventilation in all its details, learning precisely what system of motors, pumps, valves, and pipes forced the fresh air down from the Overworld and distributed it throughout Wu, somewhat as the lungs distribute oxygen to the body. Being an engineer not only by profession but by inclination, I made a more careful study of the details than duty required, until I had mastered the facts as a watchmaker masters the mechanism of a clock.

It did, indeed, occur to me that by exploring the ventilating connections with the outer world, I might find a way to escape. However, remembering my harrowing experiences on my first attempt at escape, and knowing that a second attempt might not end so fortunately, I decided to bide my time.

Had it not been for one fact, I should have found life as Ventilating Inspector almost pleasant. The blot on the landscape was the menace of Loa. Not even by removing to the Ventilation Dormitory could I relieve myself of her attentions. Of course, I avoided her whenever possible—but before I had been working in my new position for ten wakes, disconcerting rumors began to reach my ears.

"Well, friend," another Inspector exclaimed one day, "we

hear you're in luck! Great caverns! How did you ever find such a lovely girl? So fat and wrinkled, they say! And the daughter of a Second Class professor! Congratulations! May you have fourteen sons, to provide a glorious turnover for your country!"

Naturally, I denied having matrimonial intentions. But my companions smiled knowingly, nudged one another, and protested, "By Thuno Flatum! You can't fool us! You've been engaged for wakes and wakes. Why, the *Screamer* announced it, issue before last."

"The *Screamer*—announced it?"

"Of course! Can't keep it a secret any longer!"

Soon after this, Loa herself visited me in the company of her father. As they had announced themselves unceremoniously in my rooms in the dormitory, they succeeded in cornering me.

I noticed that she was eyeing me reproachfully; for a moment the wild hope came to me that she was angry and had come to release me from the entanglement.

"Why haven't you come to see me, dear?" she began accusingly, but in a manner that showed her willingness to be magnanimous.

"Now, Loa darling," remonstrated the Professor, "haven't I told you a thousand times it isn't becoming for a Third Class man to call on a Second Class lady? No, not even when they're engaged! So, of course, Loa, you must come to him instead. He had a right to feel offended at *your* neglect."

But I confessed to feeling no offense, and Loa advanced toward me with a smile. "See, dear, what I have for you," she announced, taking a gleaming object from her handbag. "It's all yours! Your wedding bracelet!"

"Wedding bracelet?" I gasped, wishing there were some convenient way to sink through the floor.

"Of course. Don't you know it's the custom for the lady to give the gentleman a bracelet?"

"Now, Loa, how could you expect him to know?" demanded Tan Torm reprovingly. "After all, he was born a barbarian, and still isn't familiar with civilized ways."

"Yes, I had forgotten," admitted Loa apologetically. "Here, dear, is the bracelet!" And while I sank down in consternation, she slipped a red-studded silver band on my left wrist.

"There, dear!" she went on rapturously. "Isn't it a beauty? It's ruby, the color of your heart's blood!"

As I snatched at the bracelet, with the idea of removing it,

I was diverted from my purpose by feeling Loa's arms about my neck; and for a moment we were locked in an embrace more satisfying, I hope, to her than to me.

It was Professor Tan Torm who, at this point, unwittingly saved the day. "Here, my dears," he said, unfolding an enormous document with a brass seal, "here, my dears, is the license! There are only a few minor details to be filled out." I do not know why, but some strange, irrational hope flashed into my heart at sight of that document. I read that I guaranteed to take Loa, the daughter of Professor Tan Torm, as my one and only legal wife; that I agreed to obey the Population Laws and produce as many sons as was possible for the benefit of the Motherland; and that I promised to rear my children and conduct my married life according to the best accepted principles of Thoughtlessness. At the bottom of the page there was a space for a notary's signature, which had not yet been added. Under Loa's name I read, written elaborately in gilded letters, "Eugenically approved"; while beneath my own name no such inscription appeared.

As delicately as I could, I called this fact to the attention of Professor Tan Torm.

"Oh, my dear boy, don't let that worry you at all! A mere formality, I assure you! A fine, stalwart man like you—even if you were born a barbarian—won't have any trouble meeting eugenic requirements. I've brought the Eugenic Inspector here with us. He's waiting now in the gallery."

While I gave a horrified gasp, the Professor went to the door, flung it open, and called to someone outside. And immediately a small chalk-face, whose tall pointed hat bore an engraved sign, "Eugenics," entered and bowed low.

"Is this the bridegroom?" he inquired, pointing at me.

"Yes, yes," acknowledged the Professor. "Come right this way! My daughter and I will withdraw, leaving you to perform the tests by yourself. We will be waiting outside."

The Inspector, who declared himself to be a practicing physician, tested my heart, my lungs, and all my other organs by means of an instrument which, upon being placed on the skin, immediately registered any pathological condition by recording the exceedingly faint electrical reactions of the body.

"My dear young man," he congratulated me, at the conclusion of the test, "it is rarely that I have come across so perfect a case! I will rate you 99 and 44/100%! From the eugenical point of view, you are Grade X!"

Probably the Inspector did not understand why I looked so downcast. He glanced at a little document across the room from him, and added, "To be sure, there are a few questions I must ask, in accordance with the law. But they are mere matters of form."

Thereupon he began to fling out scores of queries, in regard to my age, my occupation, my father's age, my mother's age, the age of my sisters, brothers, cousins, aunts, uncles, grandparents, great-grandparents, etc., when they were turned over. To all these questions, I replied as best I could; and always he would nod with a pleased "Very good!" and congratulate me on my record.

At last he came to the final question. "Military experience? Military experience of your father, grandfathers, and great-grandfathers?"

"Well," said I, "I was too young to serve at the time of the First World War, and my country was trying to keep out of the Second World War when I came down here. My father never was in any war; neither were my grandfathers or great-grandfathers, so far as I know."

The Inspector shot out of his seat. "What? Your family has never been to war? It has no military record at all?"

"My family were all distinguished scholars and scientists."

"Scholars and scientists?" he flung back scornfully. "Is that all? When did they ever fight for their country? How can you expect, young man, to bring forth a capable progeny to be turned over in the next war unless you have a good fighting ancestry?"

Before this question I remained mute; hope was beginning to well up in my heart.

"No, sir," the Inspector said, "I cannot approve of you as eugenic. To permit your marriage would be to foster racial and national weakness; to encourage the growth of an unfit, noncombatant population! I regret it very much, sir, but I must stamp your application, 'Disapproved!'"

And, with that, he made a contemptuous bow and went stamping out of the room.

A few minutes later, after Loa had left my apartment with heartbroken sobs, I blessed my father and my father's fathers for having had no fighting experience!

14. THE VENTILATION THROW-DOWN

The wakes went by and gathered into months; the months lengthened into a year; and still I performed my duties as Ventilation Inspector, and could discover no way of escape to the Overworld. Then all at once, my life underwent an extraordinary change.

The occasion was one of those periodic work stoppages which menace the economic security of Wu and enable the people to enjoy the perils of warfare even when war has not been officially declared. On this particular occasion, the "throwdown" was especially dangerous; for the ventilation employees were determined to leave work. The uprising had become so serious that Dictator Thuno Flatum was said to have interrupted a fishing expedition for nearly an hour while he debated the situation with high officials.

Personally, I took the gravest view of developments, for the Ventilation Brotherhood, composed of fifty thousand workers, had issued the following ultimatum:

To the Directors of the Ventilation Company of Wu, Unlimited, we pay our respects, and submit that

Within three wakes, they must grant all our demands, or we will turn off the country's air.

Not a ventilation wheel will turn, not a breath of fresh air will blow until our terms are complied with.

If thousands of citizens, including many First Class men and women, should be suffocated as a result, we shall profoundly regret their turnover, but this is a business matter, and sentimental considerations, naturally, cannot deter us.

The demands of the strikers—mostly Third Class citizens —were as follows:

1. That wages be high enough to permit the men to eat every other wake.

2. That hours be short enough to permit them to sleep every other night.

3. That the company supply free air to the homes of all its employees.

These demands—which were variously branded by officials of the company as "inordinate," "preposterous," and "impossible"—were condemned in no uncertain terms by all First Class citizens, who pointed out that, should their terms be met, the Ventilation Company would have to raise the price of air in order to continue to pay its stockholders their present return of eleven per cent.

"The arrogance of the people knows no limits!" stated one high dignitary. "If we were to grant these exactions, the next thing they would ask would be separate living quarters for each family, or Grade X air, or reduction of taxes on the food, clothing, and water of the Third Class! Doubtless they would expect the First Class, who are legally tax-exempt, to meet these bills! No! Obviously such insubordination must be checked before it poisons the entire life of society."

This sentiment being echoed by First Class citizens everywhere, a battle to the finish was promised. "We will smother rather than submit!" rang out the defiance of the rulers. . . . "Then we will all smother together!" thundered the strikers. Already, two wakes before the expiration of the ultimatum, serious complications were reported; dozens of "throw-downers," going quietly about their way bearing banners, "We demand a breathing wage!" had been shot by the Overhears, for what the *Screamer* denounced as "their treasonous and seditious interference with business."

I myself had but little interest in the throw-down; my work was fairly easy, my wages were fairly good. Besides, I had had the temerity to consult a historical reference work, and knew that ventilation throw-downs had been occurring at intervals of about thirty years for centuries. In every case, hundreds of thousands of persons had perished as a result of interference with the air supply; while the throw-downers, if they had been able to do a few simple sums in arithmetic, would have found that they had lost more during each interval of idleness than they had gained by the inevitable settlement.

As the time approached for the throw-downers to put their ultimatum into effect, I could see how excited the people were growing. Business had come to a standstill; along avenues once crowded with dashing vehicles, the scoots had almost ceased to run; in every side-gallery I observed little knots of chalk-faces anxiously talking.

"And so you think they will really start a throw-down?" one would ask. . . . "I'm afraid so," another would reply. "I stored up containers of oxygen months ago, for just such an emergency!" . . . "What's the army for? The Government has saved our heroic warriors for just this occasion!"

Meanwhile the *Screamer* reported that Dictator Thuno Flatum was still enjoying his fishing expedition. He had caught a seven-ounce minnow by means of a new magnetic fishing reel.

At the beginning of the wake on which the ultimatum expired, I reported for work as usual at the Ventilation Office. To my surprise, the place was almost deserted; only a worn old drudge of a janitress, languidly mopping the floor, greeted me upon my arrival.

"Glorious abysses, young man!" she gasped. "Don't you care about being turned over?"

"Don't I care about being turned over?"

"By Thuno Flatum! you won't last long if those throw-downers find you! They wouldn't do anything to me, for I'm only a useless old woman. But you, sir—they'd sweep the floor with you for not joining the throw-down!"

"Oh, I know how to defend myself!"

"Think so?" she shot out. "Well, then you ought to see what they did to my neighbor, young Mr. Tu Tynn. He was as big and strong a man as you ever saw—took all the prizes in games and wrestling. Well, he wouldn't join the water workers when they threw down year before last, and—" Abruptly she halted. I saw her staring toward the door, surprise and fear in her eyes.

Wheeling about, I observed half a dozen ugly-looking men entering. On their breasts were prominent banners, reading, "Ventilation Throw-Down. Sub-committee #116."

With a threatening expression, the newcomers drew near. "We were just looking around to see that no one was working!" said the leader. "You know, brother, it isn't good for the health to be working nowadays."

Steadily I eyed the man, and deliberately drew a step nearer.

"I give you a fair chance, brother," he growled, "if you want to walk out of here without being turned over—"

Suddenly I had resolved on my course. Striding forward before the man could finish his sentence, I put my full one hundred and seventy pounds into an uppercut that caught him squarely on the chin and sent him reeling.

As he fell, I followed up my advantage. Being now within arm's length of his companions, I began to rain blow upon blow, which, because of their defective vision for things close at hand, they were unable to guard against. In less time than it takes to recount, three of the men had followed their leader to the floor. The remaining two rushed off in a panic.

With admiration and wonder, the scrubwoman stared at me as I returned from the encounter.

"Great caverns! If only Tu Tynn could have fought like that!" she sighed. "I would advise you to look out, sir. They'll see that you're turned over, if they have to bring out a whole throw-down brigade."

"Let them do their worst!" I snorted. And I sat down, crossed my legs, and awaited developments.

Less than twenty minutes later, a second Throw-Down Subcommittee arrived. Its members were eight in number, and their swaggering hostility was such that I had no difficulty in repeating my previous tactics. Before they realized what I was about, I had gotten too close for them to see clearly; and I aimed my blows so accurately that, in less than a minute, half the gang lay stretched upon the floor. The others, not quite realizing what had struck them, were quick about resorting to that discretion which most men prefer to valor. Dashing to the door, they leapt upon their scoots and darted away.

I returned to my seat in the Ventilation Office and quietly awaited the next development.

Not being good at presaging the future, I could not have known how the news of my exploit was to spread. As luck would have it, a reporter for the *Blare* happened to be outside. He had no hesitation about accepting the word of onlookers who knew as little about the affair as he did. Consequently, he radioed his paper a story that appeared in red ink all over the front page, while the other news items were driven to footnotes on back pages.

This article, which is too long to repeat in its entirety, was to the effect that a regiment of "anti-throw-down men" had appeared—no one knew where from—under the leadership of a redoubtable giant capable of turning over any adversary at a blow.

Now the speed of the papers of Wu in printing the news is phenomenal; a matter of only minutes need elapse between the occurrence of an event and its appearance in print. In fact, the *Screamer*, in a special "raid," as the natives call it, once announced the death of a high official—and printed his obituary—seventeen minutes before he actually expired.

Hence it is not surprising that, less than half an hour after I had routed the second Subcommittee, papers telling of the exploit were being flaunted in all the main galleries by the newsgirls (there were no newsboys, all the boys having gone to war). The *Blare*, like all the other papers, was owned by a group of First Class citizens, and therefore was profoundly eager to play up any account unfavorable to the throw-downers.

Even so, the article's effect would not have been possible had it not been for one weakness of the people of Wu. In most ways, they are not a credulous folk—indeed, you may show them a plain fact ninety-nine ways without convincing them; but when a statement is in print, they consider it to be beyond challenge. It would never occur to them to question any statement once it has been subjected to the sacred art of typography. As a consequence, the rumor of my prowess, once it had attained the dignity of a place in the *Blare*, had taken on the sanctity of established knowledge.

In view of the fact that the circulation of the *Blare* was somewhere in the millions (it was compulsory reading for all persons with a mental age of twelve or under), not an hour had passed before I, along with my imagined regiment of supporters, had become a subject of discussion for all Wu. And the effect upon the throw-downers may be imagined. The members of the Central Throw-Down Committee began to fear that their movement would collapse.

It was only about two hours after the little episode between myself and the second Throw-Down Committee; and I was lounging in my chair in the Ventilation Office, finding things becoming just a little boresome. The heavy air, growing hot and foul now that the ventilation had been turned off, was telling upon my nerves. I would have welcomed the appearance of another Subcommittee!

But no Subcommittee called. Evidently none could be found to meet me face to face! Instead, I was startled to hear a rattling sound in a pneumatic tube just to my right, and to note the arrival of a letter in a little steel container:

TO WHOMEVER IT MAY CONCERN:
But most of all, to the anti-throw-downer who has been decimating our men with an army corps of hired thugs,
We extend our greetings, and suggest that you immediately withdraw with your horde of brigands.

If you do not see fit to comply with this recommendation before the close of the present wake, and to surrender your arms and position, we shall make a complete turn-over of you and your ruffians.

Yours, with many remembrances of the day,

THE CENTRAL THROW-DOWN COMMITTEE
(By order of the Grand Commander of the Brass Legion of Wu)

I must confess that I read these words not without a shudder. The members of the Brass Legion had had long experience in crime. It seemed possible that they would make good their threat—perhaps by means of Mulflar—and speedily "turn me over."

However, I had gone too far to retreat. After thinking the matter over for a few minutes, I came to the conclusion that, as I had little actual power, my only hope lay in a good old-fashioned bluff.

And so I wrote the following message:

TO THE CENTRAL THROW-DOWN COMMITTEE:

I thank you for your respected communication, and for your greetings, which I return herewith.

I beg leave to inform you that I have no intention of withdrawing with my host of patriotic followers. I suggest, for my part, that you send in peace terms and settle the Ventilation Throw-Down immediately.

Should you not do so, I shall lose no time about giving proper manifestation of my wrath.

Yours, with the utmost courtesy,
HIGH CHIEF COMMANDER
CITIZENS' ANTI-THROW-DOWN
LEAGUE

Having awarded myself this title as a final stroke, I dispatched the letter through a pneumatic tube.

15. TO DREAM UPON THE THRONE . . .

In spite of throw-downs and minor catastrophes, the war between Wu and Zu was still being waged. Of late, however, it had grown dull; except for the periodic capture and recapture of a few square yards, and the daily turnover of several thousand men on each side, nothing was happening.

Nevertheless, Zu had not forgotten that they were still fighting; and when they heard of the ventilation trouble in Wu, they vowed to take advantage of the opportunity. In order to accomplish this end, they resorted to the Subterrains, those formidable machines which bored underground and attacked by means of Mulflar torpedoes.

The result was that, on the day the throw-down was officially declared, half a dozen Subterrain assaults were launched throughout Wu; the turnover, according to treaty, was limited to Second and Third Class citizens. But the facts were not known until long afterwards, and then only imperfectly; hence the explosion that wrecked the headquarters of the Central Throw-Down Committee was not generally ascribed to its actual source.

The Head of the Committee was known to have received my letter of defiance, and had just called his secretary to dictate an order which would end my revolt once for all, when suddenly the earth rose beneath his feet. He and a corps of his assailants were turned over in a disaster that left their offices a charred heap of ruins.

Naturally, the *Blare* and the *Screamer* were delighted to report the tragedy; and having already learned of my letter to the Committee, the editors of both journals concluded that the occasion called for another "Extra-extra." The position taken by the two editors was identical: that the blow had been struck by the "Citizens' Anti-Throw-Down Committee," whose "High Chief Commander" was fulfilling his promise to give a "manifestation of his wrath."

Actually, the attack upon the headquarters of the Central Committee would have ended the throw-down in any event. Deprived of their leaders, the throw-downers would have been disorganized; and disorganization would have led to the collapse of the whole movement. But no one even thought of disagreeing with the *Blare* and the *Screamer*, which gave me the entire credit for the accomplishment. Not half a dozen hours after the Subterrain attack, the throw-down was officially over.

Even while the throw-down was being settled, I received a visit from a distinguished delegation. I was still seated in the Ventilation Office, gnawing at a lunch of concentrated food capsules and amusing myself by reading the *Screamer*'s story of my alleged exploits, when the blast of a whistle at the door made me leap up.

Riding toward me on scoots decorated with green and vermilion, and surrounded by dozens of mincing lackeys, were three chalk-faces whose shriveled forms, profuse adornments, and artificial eyes, ears and breathing apparatus proclaimed them to be First Class citizens.

In accordance with the requirements of good form, I bowed low, sweeping the floor with the palm of my hand as a sign of deference; but without acknowledging my bow, one of the First Class men lifted a megaphone to his mouth and addressed me abruptly, as was deemed only proper in the presence of a menial:

"Tell me, sir, are you the High Chief Commander of the Citizens' Anti-Throw-Down Committee?"

I mumbled in the affirmative.

The entire procession had come to a halt at a distance of about twenty feet, and I could see how the three First Class citizens were turning their telescope-like eyepieces in my direction.

"You have done a noble service in the cause of your country and the First Class," continued my interlocutor. "I shall not question you too minutely on your methods, lest they prove—well, shall we say in violation of the letter of the Criminal Code? Allow me to introduce myself, sir, as the thirteenth Vice-Executive Director of the Ventilation Company."

Once more I bowed low, taking care to sweep the floor with the palm of one hand.

"And I," testified the second First Class man, also through a megaphone, "am one of the seventeen Political Settlers of the Ventilation Company."

"Political Settlers?"

"Yes, indeed!" stated the man, looking a little offended at

my ignorance. "Very important work we do, too! It is our business to settle things with politicians and political job sellers."

"And I, sir," the third of my First Class visitors informed me with a blare of his megaphone, "am the Senatorial Representative of the Ventilation Company."

"Senatorial what?"

"Senatorial Representative. The delegate elected by the Ventilation Company, in accordance with law, to represent its interests in the Senate. Don't you know, sir, that every concern doing a business of more than eleven millions annually is entitled to have a representative in the Senate?"

"And to what, gentlemen, do I owe the honor of this visit?"

It was the thirteenth Vice-Executive Director who undertook to reply:

"You may well ask that question, sir. Not once in ten thousand wakes is a Third Class citizen, such as you appear to be, flattered with a visit from the First Class. But your case, sir, is exceptional. Owing to your unusual services on behalf of the Anti-Throw-Downers, we have been appointed by the Directors of the Ventilation Company as a committee of three to express our personal approval and appreciation."

"I thank you, gentlemen," said I, once more bowing low, but wondering if the visitors had gone through all this hocus-pocus merely in order to express an empty commendation.

"You are the sort of man, sir, that we like to have in our employ," announced the Political Settler. "Your talents are being wasted—thrown away—here in this Third Class office. We have decided to elevate you to a more worthy post."

"Yes, sir," the Senatorial Representative took up the report, "we will appoint you to the Engineering Department. As Ventilating Engineer, you will have charge of two thousand employees, who will be subject to your orders in all things!"

This time, when I bowed to the floor, it was as an expression of sincere gratitude.

"There is only one difficulty," the thirteenth Vice-Executive Director bewailed, shaking his head ruefully. "The law forbids appointment to the Engineering Department of anyone except a First or Second Class citizen."

"Well, after all, I don't insist on staying Third Class!"

The Political Settler beamed upon me, and drew his eyepieces a little closer against his wizened face. "Just what I was thinking!" he declared. "I knew you wouldn't insist on staying Third Class. By Thuno Flatum! When there's a politician, there's a way—as the ancient saying goes. The law distinctly says that no Third Class citizen shall ever become Second Class; but we'll prove to the courts that you really were Second Class all along. Leave that to me, sir—as a Political Settler, that's my specialty."

I bowed gratefully once more, and assured the man that I had always felt misplaced in the Third Class.

But even as I spoke, a new doubt overcame me. Perhaps there was some hidden flaw in the offer! Perhaps I should have to pay a heavy fee for being made Second Class, or should be taxed beyond my capacity! And so I promptly put some questions on these points.

If it had been possible for First Class citizens to laugh, my hearers would surely have done so. As it was, a sound like a dry rattle issued from their thin lips.

"Pay a tax for being made Second Class?" growled the Senatorial Representative. "Great caverns! Quite the contrary! My colleagues and I have taken care of that. Why, sir, you will get a refund for the taxes you paid in the Third Class!"

"How can that be?"

"It's very simple. Taxation, as all authorities agree, should be placed where it bears least heavily. Now there are ten times as many Third Class citizens as First and Second class combined, so naturally they are much more able to bear the weight of taxation. Therefore all taxes are placed on the Third Class."

Now I had not always admired the logic of the chalk-faces; but on this occasion, it seemed to me that there was something to be said for their reasoning.

"Only one thing more!" continued the Political Settler. "There's the matter of your salary. Considering that you won't have any more taxes to pay, I trust you will find it sufficient to have your present remuneration quadrupled."

For a moment I stood gaping at my benefactor, wondering if he were trying to make sport of me.

"Well, sir, I don't blame you for being in doubt," sympathized the thirteenth Vice-Executive Director. "After all, you should really get more than that, in order to keep up your Second Class position. I'll speak to the other Directors and see if they can't do something better for you. Perhaps they'll consent to voting you an annual bonus, also tax-free. Meanwhile you may report for work the wake after next."

"Thank you, thank you exceedingly!" I acknowledged, bowing to the floor for about the twentieth time.

Then, while my visitors uttered sharp orders to their lackeys and wheeled ceremoniously away, I sank down upon my chair in astonishment.

The duties and obligations of my new position were formidable—if you looked at them merely on paper. I was the official possessor of seven titles and subtitles, from Supervising Engineer to Sub-Director of the Airways; I was the occupant of a capacious suite of rooms, with a huge private office marked HOURS BY APPOINTMENT ONLY; I had the promised two thousand employees, from office girls to Ventilating Linemen, all of them strictly at my bid and call; and I was provided with whole libraries of literature, and a list of 55 Everyday Rules, which I was told I must follow scrupulously.

However, I hardly glanced at these rules, and never so much as turned the pages of the instruction books; for I found that my assistants, at less than a tenth of my salary, did all the work, while my only task of any consequence was to sign my paycheck every five wakes. This, naturally, left me with much time on my hands. But I did not waste my hours; I devoted them to enlarging my knowledge of the ventilation system, until there was no man in all Wu who understood the apparatus so thoroughly as I.

Despite my good fortune—good fortune that made me the envy not only of the Third Class, but of thousands in the Second Class—I was still not contented. There was the dread of encountering Loa, whom I had not seen since being declared eugenically unfit. From time to time I ran across Professor Tan Torm. He would look at me with a reproachful air and inquire, "Why don't you come round to the house sometime, my boy? Loa has been asking about you. Now that you are Second Class, like us, it can no longer be class delicacy that keeps you away." I would apologize, make some excuse—the pressure of work, etc.—and promise to pay him a visit as soon as I was able.

Day by day, I was growing wearier of the Underworld, and its network of galleries and chasms illuminated with the weird greenish-yellow light. My thoughts were constantly upon means and opportunities of escape, but I still was hopelessly imprisoned. The only connection between the Underworld and the Overworld was by means of the ventilating tubes, some of which admitted the fresh air from above, and others of which were the outlet for used and vitiated air, and all these vents had been placed under a military guard.

Before I had been Ventilating Engineer for many wakes, I began to turn my attention to a vast project. The idea had first been put into my mind by the Ventilation Throw-downers; and while in the beginning it had seemed too fantastic for consideration, the thought kept recurring. At length I weighed its advantages dispassionately, and decided that it was not so impracticable as it had seemed.

During my investigation of the air system, I had come across a certain little wheel, rusty with age, which I had turned with surprising results. Upon being jerked slightly to the right, this wheel set in operation an electric current, which released a steel partition in the central ventilating tube, blocking the channel somewhat as the human breathing apparatus would be blocked by a pebble in the windpipe. It was quite by accident that I had made the discovery, and at first I had merely amused myself by choking the ventilation for periods of a few seconds each—not long enough for the effects to be noticed.

But gradually, as I toyed with the wheel, a startling realization came to me. Its rusted condition showed that it had not been used recently; indeed, it may have been neglected for decades or even centuries. Was it not likely that the chalk-faces, because of their inability to see clearly close at hand, had overlooked its existence?

The wheel, located in an unfrequented side-gallery a few hundred yards from my office, now became the crux of my scheme. Suppose that I were to stage a private throw-down! Did I not have all the resources at my disposal? And would I not be helped by the reputation which those anti-throw-down organs, the *Blare* and the *Screamer*, had unwittingly built up for me?

"The gains justify the pains!" I told myself, quoting an old precept of the chalk-faces; and, fortified by this high moral axiom, I decided to take the plunge.

A day or two later, all Wu was cast into a furore. Another ventilation throw-down had been declared, stated the *Blare* and the *Screamer* in a series of "Super-extra-extras." The air supply had been cut off entirely! And no one knew who the throw-downers were or what they demanded.

16. THE ULTIMATUM

Two wakes had gone by without ventilation. The land of Wu was in a state of disorder compared with which the disturbances of the previous throw-down were as nothing. The present outbreak did not seem to involve any principle at all; it merely meant suffering. The people were both frightened and indignant, and had no hesitation about blaming the Government.

Consequently, the Second and Third Class citizens, though usually meek as babes owing to their thoughtlessness, were becoming unruly. They gathered in wild bands and processions, parading through the First Class districts and shouting, "We want air! We want air!" They stormed at the doors of the Ventilation Company, and even at the palace of Thuno Flatum. "Air for our children! Air for our children!"

And as if such radical declarations were not sufficient, some of the ardent air-lovers burst out in riots, wherein, on several occasions, more than one First Class citizen had to flee for his life. The insurrectionists, to be sure, were always suppressed by the police, who made excellent use of the sneeze-gas bomb (a clever little weapon which produced the equivalent of a severe attack of hay fever).

Now I must confess that, after two wakes, the state of the public galleries was deplorable. The atmosphere, stagnant, hot, and heavy, reminded me of nothing so much as of a New York subway at rush hours; the depletion of the oxygen had advanced so far that many persons were complaining of headaches, while many others felt as languid and dull as if drugged. Plainly, matters were becoming serious.

While the whole country was being reduced to a state of acute distress, no one as yet suspected the source of the trouble. But I was moving toward my objective. As soon as the throw-down began, I dispatched a message to Dictator Thuno Flatum through one of those pneumatic tubes which provide automatic mail service throughout Wu; and since there was no way of tracing any letter back to its point of origin amid the ramifications of the postal system, I knew that I was perfectly safe in this course. At the same time, I took care that

Thuno Flatum's reply should reach me in a manner equally safe.

The following was my message:

To His Abysmal Excellency
Thumo Flatum
First of the First Class
Prime Dictator and High Chief Potentate of Wu:

Greetings, along with a humble word from one of your subjects. The air has been turned off, and will remain off until such time as I decide to turn it on again. If, in the meanwhile, you wish the ventilation restored, kindly announce in the Blare or the Screamer when and where you will grant me an audience. Before our meeting can take place, you must guarantee, on your word of honor and that of your ancestors, not to permit me to be molested in any way. Should this condition be violated, the country will remain airless forever.

Yours militantly,
President, Better Air Association

On the following wake, I dispatched a similar message, and again on the third wake; while Thuno Flatum, with characteristic stubbornness, again withheld a reply. He had had the poor discretion, however, to give out my letters to the newspapers. Hence both the *Blare* and the *Screamer*, on three successive wakes, reproduced my communications in full, commenting that they were obviously the work of a madman.

Meanwhile the officers of the Ventilation Company had turned from their customary task of counting dividends in order to try to trace the reason for the lack of ventilation. All the inspectors and engineers were made to work overtime; I myself, much to my amusement, was instructed to exert myself diligently to locate the trouble. Of course, I made a great show of seeming to comply, and bustled about my headquarters officiously, flinging out orders by the dozen and sending off my subordinates to search in places where I knew they would find nothing.

By the third wake, the directors of the Ventilation Company were in despair. Thuno Flatum and other high officers of state were said to be wearing a worried expression; the Dictator, returned from his minnow-fishing, had canceled an engagement to play poli-boli, an athletic game, performed with marbles, especially popular with First Class citizens; and riots were breaking out in scores of widely scattered places.

The *Blare* now reversed its attitude and advised the Dictator to see "the madman who insolently terms himself President of the Better Air Association." Conditions were becoming so critical, the paper pointed out, that it would be wise to clutch at any straw; indeed, the scarcity of air was ruining business, as was evident from the fact that bank clearings had gone down seventy-five per cent in the past two wakes. If the throw-down continued another three or four wakes, the cost might well rise as high as 100,000,000 brass fingers. The possible cost in life was not mentioned.

The argument of the *Blare*, as might have been foreseen, proved unanswerable.

Immediately I began making preparations for the inevitable meeting. It was not half an hour later, when a new edition of the *Blare* declared that Thuno Flatum was awaiting my visit, and, in fact, had high hopes that our interview would end the throw-down. And it was but a few minutes after reading this announcement that I prepared to set out for the Dictator's palace.

I did not, however, go alone. To appear before the sovereign unattended would be neither wise nor safe, particularly since I had to present a proposal which, to say the least, was audacious. I decided to pick an escort of, say, about three or four hundred of the most muscular-looking employees at my call.

To be sure, I must not take any of my attendants into my confidence, or let them suspect what I was attempting. But such was their stage of trained thoughtlessness that it was simple to keep the truth from them. Besides, there was the concoction known as the "muffler," which employers had been wont to feed to employees, so that the victims could take orders with mechanical perfection, but were incapable of knowing, thinking, or feeling.

As the Ventilation Company always had a large supply of this drug on hand, I fed it to about four hundred of my followers; then I ordered them all to take their places at once in scoots and follow me.

With this magnificent array of supporters, I looked forward eagerly to my visit to Thuno Flatum.

Realizing that I was attempting an experiment which might lead to disaster, I took one or two simple precautions. The first was to disguise myself, for I did not want it known that it was a "colored barbarian" who was challenging the throne of the Dictator. The disguise was accomplished easily enough, largely by means of a chalky powder with which I made my face milky-pale; in addition, I used a pair of heavy amber glasses, so as to conceal the gray of my eyes; and I steeped my hair in an ashen dye. Thus equipped, I was hardly to be distinguished from the average man of Wu.

But as I drew near the Dictator's headquarters, I took another precaution. I dropped back toward the rear of the procession, after giving instructions as to where my associates were to proceed. And well that I did so! When we had come within half a mile of the brilliant cavern where Thuno Flatum held court, we were impeded by a rabble who flung stones and epithets, and distributed some sneeze-gas bombs, by which half a score of my followers were disabled.

Fortunately, I myself was unharmed; and a few minutes later I arrived, with the majority of my followers, in that great hall which I so well remembered from my previous visit to the Dictator.

But how different was this arrival from my previous visit! Then I had been forced to approach the sovereign on all fours, waiting impatiently until his Lordship should condescend to notice my existence. But today I marched boldly forward, with no hint of deference; and my attendants, reduced to such a state of thoughtlessness that they did not know themselves to be in the presence of Thuno Flatum, unquestioningly followed my example. Not until I was at the very pedestal of the throne did I pause; and then it was without any sign of submission.

"Thuno Flatum," I announced, "I come at your summons, as the President of the Better Air Association!"

It was easy to see that my words had produced consternation. The helmeted guards unbent from their stony rigidity sufficiently to allow the pikes to tremble in their hands; the body servants of Thuno Flatum forgot their attentions to their regal master in order to stare at me in petrified unbelief. And a group of spectators, doing obeisance upon their hands and knees, collapsed with surprise.

The monarch himself seemed dumbfounded, and leaned forward in his chair until I feared he would fall out. It was a moment before any of his attendants could recover themselves sufficiently to lift the megaphone to his mouth.

"What is that you say?" he squealed. "Do you not know

that you are addressing the Prime Dictator and High Chief Potentate of Wu?"

"To be sure, Your Abysmal Excellency, that is why I am here," I returned suavely. "It would hardly suit my purpose to waste time on any lesser official."

His puny little form shook with such wrath that not until his attendants had fanned him for five minutes and applied doses of cold water was he able to find words again.

"Who are you, to speak to me in this manner? Your tones are the uncultivated ones of some Third Class rubbish! Do you not realize that you have been guilty of an offense worse than treason—a felony for which better men than you have been executed—the crime of Contempt of the First Class?"

Exhausted with the effort of this long speech, Thuno Flatum had to be fanned again by his lackeys and allowed several minutes in which to recuperate.

"What's to prevent me from punishing your insolence?" he finally resumed.

Through the mirrors, I could see how the guards behind me began to creep forward, with their pikes pointed menacingly in my direction. I knew that I had no course except to be bold. "Punish me, if you wish, Your Abysmal Excellency," I challenged, "but my followers cannot be disposed of so easily. Those you see here are as nothing to the hosts waiting to avenge me."

"What do I care for your followers?" snapped Thuno Flatum. "You cannot cow me with threats! Men of my Class have ruled for a hundred generations, and there has never been a revolt!"

"All the more reason for having one now!" I insisted. "Think, Your Abysmal Excellency, what power I hold! I am more precious to you and your people than a thousand times my weight in brass!"

I could see the guards still creeping forward. Also, I could detect a gleam of mirth in the salmon eyes of some of the spectators, and realized that my words had not been taken so seriously as I could have wished.

But my trump card was still up my sleeve. "Remember, Your Abysmal Excellency," I warned, "only one man in all Wu is able to restore your ventilation. If I perish, the secret perishes with me, and you will all be turned over by lack of air."

Half-suppressed groans from the spectators, and from Thuno's attendants, showed that this bolt had struck home.

"How do I know you speak truth?" demanded the Dictator.

"Test me, Your Abysmal Excellency. If you will agree to my terms, I will restore the ventilation at any moment you stipulate."

"You talk like a madman!" barked my opponent through his megaphone. And then, after a moment's hesitation, "Still —still, I am broadminded. There can be no harm in hearing your offer. If you do not keep your promise, there will always be time for punishment. What are your terms?"

"Your Abysmal Excellency," I began, "according to all reports, you have ruled long and notably. You have performed great services for the First Class and for your country. But it is not fair that any man, however willing, be harnessed too long with the yoke of state. After a time, his shoulders should be relieved of the burden, so that he may enjoy the pleasures of private life. It is for this reason, Your Abysmal Excellency—"

At this point, my speech was rudely halted. A blast of the Dictator's megaphone rang through the audience chamber, and Thuno Flatum, straining forward with quivering form, and face that had turned all colors from white to purple, staggered out of his seat in his rage, shook his midget fist at me, and collapsed.

It was several minutes before his attendants could fan him back to life.

"Great caverns!" he squeaked through the megaphone, after being restored to himself. "What is that you suggest? Do you have the daring, the effrontery, to ask that I—that I step down—" Choked by the fury of his own words, he was unable to continue.

An uneasy glance at the mirrors showed me the guards still creeping up from behind, while my followers still made way before them. "Your Abysmal Excellency," I said hastily, "you have caught my idea. For the good of your country and the restoration of ventilation, it is time that you step down, and that I step up—"

By now, the Dictator had regained his breath sufficiently to interrupt me by bellowing through the megaphone: "So, now we have your terms, have we? You would displace me on the throne? Me—Thuno Flatum, the High Chief Potentate of Wu! Seize him, guards! Seize him!"

Before I had time to leap aside, I felt heavy arms about my

shoulders, and was pinned in the iron grip of three guardsmen.

Though ready to collapse once more with the effort of so much speaking, Thuno Flatum was able to scream:

"Take him away! Away! At once! Waste no time! I'll sign the death warrant!"

Vainly I strove to command my followers; to order them to my rescue. But something had gone wrong with the operation of the drug; and, automatons that they were, they seemed powerless to obey.

As the guards started to drag me me off, I saw how excitedly the Dictator's twenty attendants were laboring to restore him to life.

"One minute!" I shouted to the guards, doing my best to give my voice that authoritative loudness which the people of Wu respect. "I must have another word with his Abysmal Excellency!"

"Take him away! Away! At once!" The ruler had recovered. "I'll sign the death warrant! We'll kill him by inches with sulphur fumes!"

While the guards started to drag me away once more, and my mind conjured up visions of suffocation by sulphur, I cried out:

"One minute, Your Excellency! Remember, if I die, you all die! Without me, the air will remain off forever!"

"Without you, the air will remain off forever?" echoed Thuno Flatum. "Then let it stay off! What do I care? Have I not my oxygen tanks?" Derisively, he pointed to the steel tanks connecting with his breathing tubes.

"So you would breathe while your prople smother?" I demanded. And then, turning to the guards, "Do your duty, men! Take me away! Thuno Flatum, your master, will still breathe oxygen while you all smother!"

The effect of these words was electrifying. One of the guards, releasing me with a hurried gesture, reached for his three-pointed helmet and flung it off, to reveal a gasping, perspiring individual close to the last stages of exhaustion.

"I'm through!" he groaned. "By the white hairs of my ancestors, I'm through! Let someone else be turned over! I'm going on a throw-down!"

"So am I!" announced a second guard, snatching off his helmet.

"So am I!" snapped a third, a fourth, and a fifth, until, in a moment, all the pike bearers stood unhelmeted and rebellious. "We're going on a throw-down! A throw-down!"

"We want air!" one of them started the cry . . . "We want air, we want air!" began to echo and reverberate through the whole great hall. And the guards, surging forward in an angry mass, lost all semblance of military order, pushing, scuffling, shouting.

For a moment, Thuno Flatum was too thunder-stricken for words. Then, as his attendants crowded about him protectively, I thought I heard his voice lifted during a brief lull in the storm: "This is sedition! Sedition! I'll have you all violet-rayed! I'll have you—"

But I did not hear the conclusion of the speech. Taking advantage of the hubbub, I started hastily toward the door, ordering my attendants to follow. The Revolution had begun!

17. LUMA THE ILLUSTRIOUS

Hardly had I escaped from Thuno Flatum's audience hall when I noticed an athletic-looking man darting from the direction of the throne room. Breaking through the ranks of my followers in a frenzy of arm-waving agitation, he headed straight toward me. "Wait a minute there! Just a minute!" he shouted, when he had come within a few dozen yards. "I've something to tell you!"

He finally caught up with me, puffing prodigiously, just as I had reached my scoot. Only then, as I turned in alarm to confront him, did I recognize the official yellow badge of the press!

"I represent the *Screamer!*" he gasped, when he had half-way regained his breath. "Let me have your story! Quick! The *Blare* man will be here any minute!"

Sure enough, another individual, racing toward us from far down the gallery, proved to be a reporter from the *Blare!*

Naturally, though still in a hurry to get away, I could find time to present my story to both newspapers, with an abundance of detail.

In less than an hour, the new editions were on sale.

"Air special! Air special!" I heard the newsgirls crying from the court outside my apartment window, as I paced back and forth, trying to decide upon my next action. Without delay, I rushed out to buy a paper; but was able to do so only with difficulty, for people were flocking from all sides to get copies. However, I did manage to procure a *Screamer*, and this is what I read:

INSOLENT STRANGER CHALLENGES
THUNO FLATUM!

MAN IN AMBER SPECTACLES WARNS,
"MAKE ME DICTATOR AND I
RESTORE AIR!"

Guards in a commotion! Back claims of audacious intruder!

There followed a highly colored account of the day's events, in which I was described as a "madman seeking to foment revolution," while Thuno Flatum was represented as "defending his position with the indomitable might and valor for which the First Class is so justly noted." It was admitted, however, that I was formidable, being backed by an army variously estimated as containing between ten thousand and a hundred thousand fanatics, of whom several thousand had accompanied me to the Dictator's throne room. In the face of such a menace, Thuno Flatum was more than courageous —so the paper said—to resist my demands, even though the country should have to remain unaired for a few wakes more.

As I glanced up from the sheet, I could see that the people around me were profoundly affected by the news. For once, it seemed, an action of Thuno Flatum's had not met with unquestioning approval.

"What's that?" I heard a chalk-face to my left growling. "So we're to stay without air, while the First Class breathe from oxygen tanks! Let's have air, I say! Air, air, air! What do I care who's on the throne, so long as we can breathe? . . . Tell me, what do you think, brother?" he demanded, turning in my direction.

"My principle," said I, "is air over all."

"Mine, too!" concurred an indignant voice from our right. "The children haven't had a good clean breath for three wakes. Let Thuno Flatum's children be turned over, if he likes! I want mine to have air!"

"So do I! So do I!" other voices joined in.

Accordingly, I was not unprepared for the events of the next few hours. Toward the close of the wake, I went out for a stroll along one of the main galleries; and seeing a crowd assembled in a great central chamber or public square, I hastened forward with the feeling that extraordinary news was abroad. I was unable to discover what had happened. Yet by mixing with the crowd and listening, I did manage to hear some interesting remarks: "Why, I thought Thuno would rule forever! . . . Where did he run to?" . . . "I don't know. They say he's hiding in the Third Class basements." . . . "But I've heard he's gone fishing." . . . "Who's at the head of things now?" . . . "No one, they say, till we get the air back."

Gradually, details became evident. Led by the revolting guards, a mob had stormed Thuno Flatum's palace and forced him to flee.

It was but a short while later that the *Blare* and the *Screamer* came out with new editions. Their version differed considerably from what I had just heard. For the benefit of his health, which had been affected by the strain of duties of state, the Dictator had been advised by his physicians to take a brief vacation, his whereabouts being concealed so that he might enjoy the greater quiet. Both papers ended with the pious hope that their good sovereign might speedily recover.

But both, at the same time, suggested that if the self-termed "President of the Better Air Association" would restore the ventilation without further delay, he would find the people ready to grant any reasonable demand.

Acting upon this hint, I dispatched immediate letters to both newspapers. At precisely four hours and a quarter after the beginning of the following wake, I would turn on the air. And, exactly one hour and a quarter later, I would appear in the Dictator's throne room, where Thuno Flatum's guards might identify me as "the mysterious stranger" of the amber spectacles. I would, of course, claim my reward immediately, and would make no guaranty for the continuance of ventilation unless all my demands were granted.

Having dispatched these messages, I yawned and settled down for a good night's sleep.

The following wake, I arose early, and carefully prepared a speech and wrote a letter, which I secreted in my pocket. Next I resumed my disguise; and then, taking care not to be seen, I made my way to the side-gallery containing the rusty old wheel that controlled the ventilation. There I waited, watch in hand, and at precisely the promised minute, I gave a turn to the wheel, and was instantly rewarded by an invigorating breeze.

Now I made my way toward Thuno Flatum's palace, where I was expected an hour and a quarter later, gathering a hundred ventilating employees about me, and ordering them to keep close to my side.

As we sped through the various corridors, I noticed that the air was again in motion; that the heavy atmosphere of the past few days was already being dissipated. And the people, observing the change, waved banners, blew horns, and beat drums.

It was with difficulty that I made my way through the long gallery, since the crowds everywhere recognized me by the amber glasses. At length, however, I did reach the throne room, where the guards acknowledged my presence by bowing till their palms scraped the floor. As befitted a superior, I seemed not to notice their salutations, but strode at a slow pace toward the center of the hall. Then, while thousands watched me in wide-mouthed amazement, I mounted the raised platform of red sandstone and stood on the throne of the Dictator.

As I reached this regal eminence, someone raised his hands and broke into cheers; and the multitude, accepting this as their signal, echoed the cries. It was long before I was able to bring order to the gathering and launch forth upon the speech I had prepared.

"Fellow citizens of the First, Second and Third Classes," I began, "this is indeed an auspicious occasion. For the first time in more than three wakes, we can all breathe freely again. At great cost of personal sacrifice and labor, I have found a way to turn on the ventilation—"

At this point another salvo of cheers broke forth.

"At great cost of personal sacrifice and labor," I resumed, "I have saved you all, my fellow citizens. For this service I claim no personal reward, since the satisfaction of rescuing my countrymen will always be a sufficient compensation. However, I have a message to deliver. It is from your Dictator, his Abysmal Excellency, Thuno Flatum."

The throng became silent; several thousand pairs of eyes and ears strained forward eagerly while, with a flourish, I removed a brass-sealed document from an inner pocket.

"Here is a letter from Thuno Flatum," I declared, knowing that the people, unable to see clearly close at hand, could not detect the falsehood. "Before I read it, let me introduce myself by the name which our beloved Dictator has always applied to me. I am called Luma the Illustrious."

"Luma the Illustrious! Hurrah! Hurrah! Hurrah for Luma the Illustrious!" thundered the mob, while hundreds bowed in token of obeisance.

"Now listen carefully to the words of Thuno Flatum!" I shouted, unfolding the letter I myself had written a few hours before.

When the crowd had once more grown silent I read in sonorous tones:

"To His Highness, Luma the Illustrious
Greetings, and heartiest regards

"Since my poor health makes it necessary for me to renounce the duties of state for a time, I wish that you, Your Highness, would rule in my place during my ab-

sence. I am confident it would be impossible to find anyone more competent than your eminent self. During my
absence, the people must grant you the same unquestioning respect and obedience they would accord to me.

    Faithfully your servant,

        "Thuno Flatum,

            "Prime Dictator and High Chief
            Potentate of Wu."

As I folded the document, a thunderstricken silence pos-
sessed the people. Then all at once they broke into an uproar
such as I had never heard before. "Long live Luma! Long
live Luma! Long live Luma the Illustrious!"

Now, as never before, I realized the advantages
of thoughtlessness; it never occurred to my hearers to question my assertions. Already I had resolved that, as Dictator,
I would make thoughtlessness compulsory.

But just as I was congratulating myself on my success, a
commotion arose at the corner nearest the entrance, and I
could see the guards swaying back and forth vigorously, as
if to throw out some troublesome intruder.

"What is it, men? What is it?" I shouted.

Momentarily the commotion ceased; while the husky voice
of one of the guards shouted back:

"Your Abysmal Excellency, what shall I do? There is a
man here who claims to be Thuno Flatum!"

At these words, I was as near to heart failure as I ever
hope to be. I could see how the crowd, awed by the magic
words "Thuno Flatum," had made way near the source of
the commotion, leaving a familiar figure to wheel toward
me on a scoot, accompanied by half a dozen attendants.

His royal garments were frayed and damaged; the purple
crest upon his head was torn and bedraggled; the green and
saffron of his uniform was soiled with muddy blotches, and
the string of huge rubies no longer dangled about his neck.
Nevertheless, I had seen enough of the Dictator to identify
him even in his present shabby plight!

"Your Abysmal Excellency, this man claims to be Thuno
Flatum!" repeated one of the guards.

"Thuno Flatum! He claims to be Thuno Flatum!" I could
hear the mob echoing in surprise.

"I *am* Thuno Flatum!" avowed the intruder, with an angry squeak through the megaphone. "I *am*—I *am* Thuno Flatum!"

I do not know what it was, in that desperate emergency, that put the saving thought into my mind. "Seize that man! Seize him!" I cried, pointing to the newcomer with a fierce simulation of anger. "It's a capital offense, to impersonate the Dictator!"

"A capital offense, a capital offense to impersonate the Dictator!" echoed the multitude.

"I am *not* impersonating the Dictator! I *am* Thuno Flatum!—the Prime Dictator and Chief Potentate of Wu!" insisted the puny figure on the scoot, while his thin right arm shook in my direction in impotent rage.

"Look at him! Just look at him! He claims to be the Prime Dictator!" I howled, and rocked back and forth in feigned mirth. "When did Thuno Flatum ever wear soiled saffron? When did he show himself without the royal rubies? Guards, seize the impostor!"

"Look at him! Look at him! Just look at him! When did Thuno Flatum ever wear soiled saffron?" yelled the mob, roaring in amusement more genuine than my own.

At the same time, the heavy arms of a guard closed about the feeble, resisting figure. "I am, I *am* Thuno Flatum!" he wailed, for the last time. "It is you, you who are the impostor, the traitor! Only listen, listen—"

He was interrupted by louder laughter than ever; the thunders of public merriment drowned out his words.

"Guards, place him in a cell!" I shouted, when the peals of mirth had begun to subside. "He is a madman! We will keep him locked up until—until Thuno Flatum returns!"

As a corps of guards disappeared down a side-passage with the manacled Dictator and his attendants, the crowd burst once more into cheers: "Long live Luma the Illustrious!"

18. THE LAST REFUGE

In order to press on to more crucial events, I shall not linger over my first few months as dictator. Clad in the magnificence of my new office, I dwelt in a spacious suite of rooms, with palatial adornments and scores of attendants; I enjoyed the applause and veneration of millions; I held court daily on the throne of Thuno Flatum, decided matters of public policy and law and issued orders which, theoretically, could be disobeyed only under pain of death.

Nevertheless, not all flowed smoothly. The Second Class and the Third never so much as inquired why Thuno Flatum was taking so long a vacation; but the First Class had not been trained to an equal degree of thoughtlessness. It was pointed out that Luma was too healthy to be First Class; his limbs were not shriveled enough, and he could actually walk long distances. His natural eyesight was good, his ears useful without hearing tubes, and his lungs capable of functioning without artificial aid; while he was neither bald nor toothless, as every "green-blooded" aristocrat should be. In other words, he was a mere nobody.

So persistent did such complaints become that I finally resolved on desperate measures. One by one, the worst offenders disappeared; after the Overhears had thus disposed of five hundred troublemakers, other First Class citizens recognized the wisdom of holding their tongues.

Meanwhile I was having other difficulties, due to my zeal to be a good dictator, as I set about to better the people's condition.

For example, there was the matter of the scoots. Shocked at the innumerable accidents which cost hundreds of lives each day, I ruled that all scoots keep to the right of the road, that green and red lights be installed to guide traffic at intersections, and that no scoot be permitted to travel faster than two miles a minute. Nothing that had occurred in centuries had created such an uproar as these innovations—even though it was found that, wherever the new rules were applied, the death rate fell more than ninety per cent.

"Luma interferes with the rights of private property!"

cried the people. "If a man owns a scoot, why can't he drive it any way he wants? Traffic laws are confiscation!"

The new rules were flouted almost as a matter of principle; men would openly boast of having offended. Violations became so frequent that, in disgust, I abandoned the law; and the people, with shouts of joy, returned to their old round of injuries and turnovers.

Remembering how vast quantities of good food and clothing had been consigned to the furnaces, I decreed that henceforth excess commodities should be distributed to the poor.

"What? Give the excess to the poor?" howled the First and Second Class. "Encourage shiftlessness and indolence? Reward improvidence and laziness? Overturn that sacred economic rule, 'He who has most shall give least'?"

Most vigorous of all were the protests of the National Food Distributors and the United Clothing Manufacturers, Unlimited.

"Your Excellency should realize," they wrote me in an open letter, published in both the *Blare* and the *Screamer*, "that the profits of business and the prosperity of the nation depend upon the scarcity of vital commodities. So long as there is scarcity—whether natural or artificial—people will pay high prices and stockholders will clip dividends; but as soon as an abundance occurs, prices will sink and dividends will correspondingly wane. Accordingly, we recommend that you rescind the law forbidding us to burn surplus products."

Naturally, I paid no heed to this appeal; but I knew that I was treading on dangerous ground. From the First and Second classes I heard renewed groans and rumblings of discontent, which, despite all the efforts of the Overhears, I could not suppress. Worst of all, the Third Class—to which I distributed vast amounts of commodities—were dissatisfied with what I gave them and clamored for more in such a chorus that I had almost more to fear from them than from the other classes.

Before a few months were over, I began to wish that I had remained safely Second Class. The order against adulteration of the air supply brought down upon me the wrath of my old employer, the Ventilation Company. My rule raising the military age of children from six to eight sent legions of patriots fuming to my palace in protest. The law that spies must receive a trial before being executed provoked widespread denunciation on the ground of its "sentimental weakness." And my enactment taxing the First and Second classes no less than the Third almost led to armed rebellion.

But before I tell of my further public difficulties, let me mention one private vexation. This was in connection with Professor Tan Torm and his daughter Loa.

I had hoped that, in my role as "Luma the Illustrious," I would be able to elude them entirely. But one day, when delivering a public address in my throne room, I chanced to notice two familiar faces among the front ranks of spectators.

It was only a few wakes later that Tan Torm, accompanied by his daughter, paid me a visit. In view of our past relationship and my feeling of indebtedness to Tan Torm, I could not refuse them an audience.

After congratulating me on my rise—which he ascribed to the training I had had at his hands—the Professor approached a delicate subject. Judging from the ogling glances which Loa cast me, it was all too evident that the magnanimous creature was willing to forgive my past rebuffs!

"How happy your success makes me, my dear boy!" said Tan Torm. "A great burden has been removed from us all. You need no longer be debarred from lifelong bliss. Loa has been faithful to you, my boy!"

"Yes, I have been faithful!" echoed the blushing damsel, her wrinkled face downcast.

"We well realize your position, my dear friend," continued the Professor, beaming. "Weighed down by cares of State, you have had no time to pay us a visit. Besides, it would be unseemly for a man in your high position to visit our humble quarters. To be sure, you might have summoned us here, but you hesitated, fearing to shock us too greatly. Is that not so, my boy?"

"Yes, that is so!" I groaned.

"You see, Loa, what a considerate lover you have! I always said you were lucky, my dear. Yes, you are lucky, both of you. I wish you—"

In desperation, I was ready to clutch at any straw. I interrupted Tan Torm hastily: "Have you forgotten the eugenics test?"

Both visitors smiled upon me benignantly, as one might smile at the recollection of sorrow outlived.

"Of course, we recall! It was one of the great griefs of our life. Poor Loa! It was seven wakes before she began to show a normal interest in her wrinkles again!"

"I didn't care what happened to me," added Loa, looking up with a demure twinkle in her eye. "Since you were lost to me, it didn't seem to matter if I lost all my fatness. But now, of course, my dearest, all that is over!"

"I don't see quite how," I replied, weakly, while a stabbing sensation seemed to take me at the heart.

"Why, it's all plain as light!" declared Tan Torm, still smiling. "Since you are now a law to yourself, declare yourself eugenically fit, and who will dare contradict you?"

All at once, I understood the disadvantages of being Dictator.

"To be sure, your former disbarment was valid enough," rambled on the Professor. "Having no military ancestry, you naturally weren't qualified to become the head of a family. But now your sons won't have to fight and be turned over—"

I do not know how or why—perhaps it was the Professor's reference to fighting—but at this point an idea leapt into my head. "All that is true," I broke in. "I have, as you declare, no fighting ancestry. Therefore, before assuming domestic happiness and responsibilities, I must justify myself. Tomorrow I lead the army to battle!"

Both the Professor and his daughter looked downhearted. "Oh, but that isn't necessary, my dear boy!" frowned the former. "You have—well, altogether too high a code of honor!"

"But, great caverns, it's unheard of! The leaders never go forth to fight!" pleaded Loa. "Their own lives are too valuable to risk."

"Ah, but I am no ordinary leader, and—my country's welfare is at stake. Would you have me shrink from the field of honor?" Suspecting that they would, I added, hastily, "Goodbye, my dear friends. Kindly give my regards to Tan Tal, Moa, and Noa."

Anxious as I had been to escape from Loa, her coming had not been the only reason for my sudden decision; I was anxious to find some way of diverting public attention. Besides, the enemy had lately attacked with new energy and resourcefulness. Already they had wrested from us a stretch of Nullnull seventeen yards deep and fifty-nine yards wide —a defeat which, though our papers did their best to conceal it, had somehow become public knowledge, vastly weakening my prestige. I realized that, if I were to regain the ground I had lost, Wu must retake the ground it had lost.

However, was I competent to lead the troops? On this subject I had no doubt at all; all our generals were so thoroughly versed in thoughtlessness that they did not seem hard to surpass.

No action since I had become Dictator evoked such enthusiasm as the announcement that I was about to command the army. The *Blare* and the *Screamer*, commending me in full-page editorials, expressed their thanks that I was ready to bring my people to "the most glorious turnover in history"; the masses, acclaiming me in wild demonstrations, cheered and celebrated until you would have thought I had already won a victory.

I must confess that my own plans were a little vague. I had become so weary of the Underworld that I did not particularly care if I should be turned over in the next engagement; however, I was determined to remain ruler while I lived, and did not hesitate to antagonize the generals by vetoing projects such as the one calling for a Subterrain of unprecedented power, which would shatter the roof above the capital of Zu, burying the city and all its people amid the ruins.

I set out on a scoot in the midst of an army of a hundred thousand picked soldiers. A magnificent display they made as we proceeded along the main avenues and galleries, the people shouting exultantly, "Have a successful turnover! Successful turnover!"

Owing to the torrential applause, my advance was greatly retarded; several wakes were consumed in the march to the depths, as the natives termed the battle front. And, during the interval, tremendous changes were afoot. We caught intimations of these in the bulletins from Zu, which stated that the enemy, terrified at my approach, were already thinking of retiring from the top-line depths.

Thanks to the happy intervention of our Propaganda Office, our agents in Zu had spread demoralizing reports; the new Dictator of Wu was represented as a giant eight feet tall, who, thanks to his amber glasses, had a supernatural faculty of seeing close at hand, and was therefore irresistible in battle.

To this day I am not certain just what changes did occur in that disturbed land. I was little prepared for the actuality, when, on the fourth wake since my departure for the depths, we reached the war area.

I recognized the region easily enough, by the tremendous chasms, such as the one which Clay and I had observed on our arrival in Wu; besides, I could everywhere read the effects of warfare.

Now it was that I began to look eagerly for the enemy, who were rumored to be in hiding hereabouts. My scouts pushed on ahead, being told to report any sign of hostile activity; while I, pitching camp in the wilderness at one corner of Nullnull, impatiently awaited the engagement which would either turn me over or make my reputation as the savior of Wu.

Unfortunately, it has been regarded as a first principle of warfare, in all lands and ages, that, in order to fight, you must have an enemy—and, in this case, where was the enemy? It now appeared that we could take all Nullnull without loss of life; but this, being against all precedent—which required a large turnover—would have gained me no glory.

I was on the point of marching on—against my better judgment, for I feared a trap—when one wake a courier dashed into camp and demanded to see me at once.

"Your Excellency—Excellency," he panted, when, having made deep obeisance, he stood before my chair, streaming with perspiration. "Your Excellency, I—I have just come from Zu!"

"Well, what of it?" I demanded impatiently.

"Oh, Your Excellency—Abysmal Excellency, the most wonderful news!"

"Well then, out with it!"

Still panting, the man paused for a moment in order to regain control of himself.

"Your Abysmal Excellency," he resumed, in a less excited manner, "there has been a revolution in Zu!"

"Revolution?" I cried, leaping to my feet.

"Indeed, Your Excellency, a great revolution! The people have risen up and driven En Yuno from the throne. It was not because of the war, Your Excellency. They say he did not give them the right capsules to eat. Now they have a new Dictator."

"Oh! And who may he be?"

"I wish I knew, Your Excellency. Nobody seems to know.

He calls himself Ra the Righteous. He is said to have the strangest looks of any man in the whole world."

"What does he look like?"

My visitor hesitated. "Well, Your Excellency, I know you will laugh. No man like him has been seen before. They say his eyes are blue. And his hair is red."

"Eyes blue? Hair red?" I reeled backwards, ready to collapse.

19. RA THE RIGHTEOUS

Hardly had the messenger left when I hastily dictated a letter:

To His Abysmal Excellency
Ra the Righteous
Dictator of Zu
   Whereas our army has been maneuvering for wakes on the outskirts of Nullnull, and has been unable to find any of your followers to turn over, we conclude that your citizens are too craven to join us in battle, and therefore demand that you cede the whole of Nullnull to us immediately and unconditionally. Otherwise, beware!
   Belligerently yours,
      Luma the Illustrious
         Prime Dictator and High Potentate of Wu

This letter was, of course, duly written on the official stationery by the court scribe, in the language used by both Wu and Zu. But underneath the formal message, to which I affixed my signature with a flourish, I added the following in English: For God's sake, Phil, is it you? If so, let's get together! Frank.

Knowing that these words would convey no meaning unless the new Dictator of Zu were my lost friend, I hurriedly delivered the letter to an envoy who, carrying the pink badge of neutrality, was allowed to traverse enemy territory unmolested.

Within a few hours, Ra the Righteous would have the communication; meanwhile copies of my message were sent to the *Blare* and the *Screamer*, which printed it conspicuously, with laudatory comments on my "firmness" and "courage."

Before the wake was over, the response was in my hands:

To His Abysmal Excellency
Luma the Illustrious
Dictator of Wu
   Whereas I have just received your missive, and have

114

read it with astonishment at your effrontery, I refuse un-
qualifiedly to accept any of your terms, and demand that
you, for your own good, cede the whole of Nullnull to
us.

Defiantly yours,
    Ra the Righteous
        Dictator Supreme and Sovereign
        Commander of Zu

It was with an amused smile that I read the above. But
almost cried out for joy at a little postscript, scribbled in
English. *Thank heaven, Frank, it's you! I'd given you up ages
ago! Meet me at the beginning of tomorrow wake at the end
of gallery 341C, at the northeast end of Nullnull. Better
come disguised. Phil.*

Hours before the brightening camp-lights had announced
the beginning of the new wake, I had risen from bed, disguised myself by means of a steel helmet and a long flowing
black robe, and slipped away through the wilderness of galleries that tunneled the borderland of Nullnull.

I well knew that the adventure was not without its perils;
yet the hope of seeing Clay more than sufficed to overcome
my fears. Guided by a flashlight, I kept on at a steady pace
through the darkness, until at length a welcome sign,
stamped in the rock of the cavern wall, announced that I
had reached gallery 341 C.

Down this thoroughfare, which wound tortuously, I proceeded at an increasing pace. It seemed as if I had traveled
miles before finally the gallery came to a dead end.

Then, as I paused, removed my helmet for the sake of
comfort and wondered whether I had passed Phil in the
dark, a vague shape withdrew from the dimness behind a
shelf of rock, and a well-remembered voice rang through
the air: "Frank!"

"Phil!" I called back; and the next moment we were grip-
ping each other's hands in a fervent clasp.

"Well, old fellow, let's have a look at you!" exclaimed
Clay at last, pulling out a flashlight and casting the rays full
upon my face. "You've changed; you're looking like your
own grandfather!"

"Years have gone by, you know," I returned, not pleased
by this compliment. "Now, let's take a look at you!"

Clay pulled down the mantle that had half hidden his

features, and I saw that his red locks were as abundant as ever—in fact, had grown long. He had also sprouted a full red beard, which added to his impressiveness; while deeply graven lines along his cheeks and brow bore evidence of recent suffering.

"Believe me, I never expected to see you again this side of eternity," declared Clay. "I thought the lightnings got you long ago, in the battle cavern when we both ran for dear life!"

"I thought they had got *you!* I never heard a word of you until yesterday."

"Nor I of you! We're going to have a good time hearing of each other's troubles. I've had my share, Frank, and you look as if you've had yours."

"Oh, I've been all right, everything considered. Let's hear your story first!"

"No, yours first!" he insisted, so I yielded. Both of us took seats on a rocky ledge as I recited the highlights of my recent adventures.

"You've sure had a time of it!" muttered Clay, when I had finished. "Ought to put it in a book when you get back! At that, I don't think you've got me beaten."

"No? What happened to you?"

Clay settled back on the ledge, as if seeking a more comfortable berth; and it was a moment before he spoke. Meantime it seemed to me that I saw, from around a bend in the gallery, a sudden flutter of light and a shadow moving. Just a sentinel on his rounds, I thought.

"Well, let's go back to when we parted," Clay began with a reminiscent drawl. "Both of us were pretty much in a hurry. I remember scampering down the main gallery, with the lightning just about missing me on every side; then I raced off along a side-gallery, where the lightning couldn't hit. I was so scared, I ran till my legs gave out. Then suddenly I noticed you were gone, and it came to me you'd either been hit or had rushed off down another side-gallery.

"So I started back, and lost my head so completely I cried out, 'Frank! Frank! Frank!' at the top of my voice. Well, I had to pay for that idiocy! It wasn't a minute before I was surrounded by white-faced savages, whooping like wild Indians; and they lost no time about tying me with wire and carting me away. Later I learned they were scouts from Zu, spying on their enemies of Wu.

"They bore me to their own country, and threw me into

a dungeon as a prisoner of war. Once or twice they were on the point of executing me, but my red hair interested them so much that they changed their minds just in time to save my neck. Finally, they decided to exhibit me in a circus as a 'Wild man from Pako'—the name they give to the center of the earth, where they thought I hailed from. But one day, owing to my ability to see close at hand, I managed to pick the circus lock and escape.

"I turned my hair white by means of some stolen dye, and whitened my face also—then I played highwayman, waylaying an obliging old gentleman and forcing him to change clothes with me so that I could pass as a native.

"By this time, I'd learned a good deal of the language, and was able to start life as a Third Class citizen, after being sponsored by an agent of the Department of Public Unemployment. He arranged to have me swallow the Oath of Fidelity and take a regular job, in return for signing over my wages for the first hundred wakes."

"Zu doesn't seem very different from Wu," I commented.

Clay laughed. "From all I can make out," he observed, "they're as much alike as the two halves of a split orange. Maybe that's why they hate each other so cordially."

"Maybe so," I concurred.

"My new work," Frank continued, "was as an employee of the Synthetic Capsule Producers, who manufacture all the country's food. All I had to do was to mix ingredients in the bread capsules, making sure they got just the right proportion of every vitamin from A to X. But being able to see close at hand, I made myself so useful I was promoted time after time, and after about a year became a Second Class citizen. All the while I was looking for a way to escape to the Overworld, but couldn't find any. I made inquiries, but no one had ever heard of any gray-eyed man like you. Well . . . the Capsule Producers still kept on promoting me, until at last I was General Distribution Manager—which means that I had pretty much the freedom of the works, without anything much to do except draw my pay. And then—then I started the Great Salt Revolt."

"Great what Revolt?"

"Salt Revolt! Haven't you heard of it? Why, it's about the biggest thing that ever happened in Zu. You see, it had struck me that these chalk-faces didn't put enough salt in their food, and you know how I've always liked salt. Well, one fine wake, I emptied a few kegs of sodium chloride into a batch of dough being made into capsules for the whole country. The results were excellent, I thought—for the first time since reaching Zu, I could enjoy my dinner. But the na- tives—you ought to've seen the faces they made when they tasted those capsules. Some of them grew deathly sick—suf- fered acute indigestion, convulsions, and other severe symp- toms; they'd been so long with only a bare pinch of salt that their systems couldn't stand the added dose.

"I tell you, I never saw such wild times. The people thought they'd been poisoned, and stormed about the Dic- tator's palace, crying, 'We want better food, better food, better food!' It was the funniest thing I ever saw."

"But, certainly, they could recognize the taste of salt! And, besides, chemists could analyze the capsules."

"No, they couldn't. They've always had their salt in such minute quantities they don't know what it tastes like. As for the chemists—of course, they made the analysis, but the people had been so well trained in thoughtlessness that they couldn't recognize the obvious. So they went right on believ- ing they'd been poisoned."

"Even so," I argued, "what was to prevent the authorities from throwing away the salted food and distributing new capsules?"

"Nothing—nothing at all!" Through the darkness, I heard a peal of laughter. "They did just as you say; but they were reckoning without me!"

"Without you?"

"Yes; you see, it had come to me that whoever controlled the food controlled the country—and I was getting tired of a second-rate position. I had access to the food vats—and I arranged to have a few more kegs of salt poured into the capsule mixture every time it was made.

"Then how the sparks did fly! When I felt it about time to strike, I circulated an anonymous letter, stating that I, and I alone, knew how to remove the poison from the food— and offering to give a demonstration. I won't weary you now, Frank, with the details; it's enough to say that, when the people found I could keep my promise and give them un- adulterated food, they threw over En Yuno and his party, whom they blamed for the bad capsules, and installed me in his place as Dictator, pledged to a policy of 'No salt in the bread!' So here I am! A wonderful sort of dictator, eh?" Once more, Clay's laughter rang merrily through the dark- ness.

"We're a beautiful pair of dictators, Phil!" I agreed, joining in his laughter.

Then abruptly, my mirth was cut short. Did I not again see a shadow shifting amid the dimness far down the gallery?

Clay, however, could see nothing, though he strained his eyes in the attempt. He slapped me heartily on the shoulder, and resumed. "Yes, we've both struck our gait at last! A lovely couple of dictators! But we shouldn't meet like this for a friendly chat. We're supposed to be enemies!"

"Deadly enemies!" I laughed.

"If we were found together, it would be treason! Dictators of rival countries aren't expected to be friends."

"Well, I'll tell you, Phil, we don't have to keep on breaking the rules, do we? Let's both chuck this dictator job and make a dash for home. I know all about the ventilation flues, and if we tried the climb by means of ropes—"

"Hold on there just a minute, Frank! What's getting into you?" he interrupted. "I've only been Dictator a few wakes, you know. I want to find out what it feels like."

"Oh, you'll find out, all right!" I predicted.

"Besides," he pursued, a little more somberly, "don't you think we ought to try to settle things down here before making our get-away? I mean, about this war. Suppose we fix up a little treaty?"

"A very good idea," I agreed.

"We'll have to split up Nullnull between Wu and Zu about fifty-fifty. Then we'll both claim a glorious victory, and the most thoughtless patriots everywhere will be satisfied. First, of course, you and I will have to conduct some diplomatic negotiations, couched in the deadliest and dullest language. Then we'll meet formally as enemies, and sign the treaty. After that, the war will be over, and everyone will go home happy."

"Splendid!" I approved.

"Well, I suppose I'd better get back to my followers." Clay rose from his ledge and took my hand in a warm grip. "Might be missed if I stayed away too long. Guess you're in the same boat. Goodbye . . . see you again soon!"

20. TOPPLING THRONES

According to our agreement, the Dictator of Zu and I lost no time about negotiating for peace. Within about thirty wakes, we had come to the stage of arranging an armistice; and Clay and I, meeting with great bluster and ceremony at the borderline of the two countries, duly affixed our signatures to the document which officially ended the war.

All this, however, was not quite so easy as it may sound; both of us were splashing in stormy waters. I was unable to keep close track of events in Zu, for the waves were dashing so threateningly about my own head that I had no time for outside affairs.

Never had any of my acts aroused such opposition as the attempt to establish peace. Even the move to tax the First and Second Classes had been less tempestuously received: the *Blare* and the *Screamer* openly condemned me as "capitulating to the enemy," and were not silenced even by my threat to suspend their publication; the people rose in mass demonstrations, shouting, "Down with Zu! Down with Zu!"

At the same time, insidious propaganda was being passed by word of mouth through every pit and gallery of the land. "What's to become of the munitions makers if we end the war? They will lose ruinously on their investments." . . . "Yes, and millions will be thrown out of work." . . . "Have we none of the ancient hardihood of our fathers? Do we pusillanimously dread to be turned over? . . . "Let's not surrender till Nullnull is wholly ours!"

And, mingled with these cries, there were exclamations about "The lofty ideals of the battle caves," "The triumph of thoughtlessness," and "The turnover to end turnovers."

I was fast approaching despair, and was even debating whether it would not be better to renew the war than to risk revolution.

Early one wake, shortly after rising from a sleepless bed, I picked up a copy of the *Screamer*, and was greeted by news that made my eyes almost bulge out of my head:

REBELLION IN ZU!
RA THE RIGHTEOUS OVERTHROWN!
COUNTRY IN A TURMOIL!

A counter-revolution broke out yesterday in Zu, owing to the charges of military authorities that Dictator Ra the Righteous was betraying his people into a disgraceful peace. Substantiating their accusations of treason against the popular interests, they produced the testimony of two sworn witnesses who asserted that one wake, shortly after Ra's accession to power, they followed him as he made his way in disguise into a remote gallery at the borderline of Nullnull. There he held an illicit conversation with one who, they say, is high in the Government circles of Wu; in fact, they claim to have identified the second man as no less a personage than our own Dictator.

This tale, which can only be held to be a gross libel so far as Luma the Illustrious is concerned, has been accepted without question by the people of Zu. As a result, they have stormed the royal palace, demanding resumption of the war and threatening the life of Ra the Righteous, who is now known as Ra the Treacherous. Ra himself is believed to have escaped. The former Dictator, En Yuno, is said to be on his way back to resume power.

It is impossible to describe with what emotion I read this account.

I rushed to my secretary and gave orders that scouts be sent out, and that if anyone answering to the description of the former Dictator of Zu was found, he was to be offered sanctuary, as a spy, in Wu.

Several anxious hours went by—hours during which, in my troubled preoccupation for Clay's welfare, I was unable to attend to the affairs of state or consider my own safety. And then, one of my palace guards approached with every evidence of excitement. After bowing to the floor in the established manner, he addressed me hastily:

"Your Abysmal Excellency, there is a vagabond outside who asks to see you. I told him it was impossible, you were tied up in a conference; but he gave me a bit of paper, and said that if I passed it to you, you would understand. He must be a madman, Your Excellency, for the paper is filled with a meaningless scrawl."

"Let me see it!" I demanded.

I am sure that the man, thoughtless though he was trained to be, was surprised to note the gasp of astonished joy with which I glanced at the paper, and the haste with which I demanded, "Show the visitor in!"

After the guard had saluted and left, I began to pace rapidly back and forth, while reading over and over again those few words in a handwriting I knew so well!

A minute later, a queer-looking figure entered. I do not wonder that the guard had called him a vagabond; his robe was ripped and torn in a hundred places, and here and there was stained with blood; a dark hood was drawn over his face, concealing the hair and features; his eyes looked out at me from behind binoculars; his long, cone-shaped hat was battered and dented as if from a scuffle, and the black glove was missing from his right hand.

My visitor waited until the guard had left; then removed the binoculars, and threw off his hood, revealing a figure familiar and yet strange.

For a moment I stared in astonishment at that closely cropped head, and that face from which every vestige of a beard had been shaved; at those eyes, deeply sunken as if from a sleepless vigil; at the drawn features, with the worn and ravaged lines.

"Phil!" I exclaimed. "Lord! I hardly recognized you!"

"No wonder!" He sank down upon a chair.

"But thank heaven, you're here at last!" I rejoiced. "You don't know how worried I was!"

"*You* don't know how worried *I* was. I ought to've taken your advice, Frank. This dictator business just doesn't agree with me!"

"How did you escape?" I asked. "The paper says—"

"Says Ra the Righteous is about done?" he interrupted. "Well, there wouldn't have been even mincemeat if that mob had gotten me. It was a mighty close call."

He paused, mopped his brow once more, and continued:

"Lordy! When I heard the rabble streaming through the streets, I had to think fast! I took just about the quickest shave of my life, cutting off my hair and whiskers. Then I pasted them on a dummy, which I placed near the palace entrance. While the mob was storming the gates, trying to get at that old scarecrow, I slipped on these binoculars and hood, dressed in servants' clothes, went out the back way, mixed with the mob, and even joined in yelling, 'Down with

Ra the Righteous!' Finally I escaped through a side-gallery, and took a scoot here. I've been at it all night! At the border of Wu I had a tussle with some sentries; that explains my nice society appearance." With a rueful grimace, he looked down at his torn, blood-spattered clothes.

"Well, don't mind that, Phil," I said, slapping him heartily on the shoulder. "I'll look out for you now! We've stuck together most of our lives, and I guess we can stick it out just a little longer!"

Only three wakes later, catastrophe struck.

During the interval, I had been sheltering Clay as best I could, trying to keep him disguised and hidden, and laying out a course of action. Many were the hurried little talks in which we decided that the only safety for either of us lay in the Overworld. However, since premature flight would be worse than none at all, we were making our plans coolly and deliberately. I had withdrawn the military guard from the tubes; I had secreted a quantity of hooks, ropes, and other climbing tackle at the base of a flue, which, I knew, led upward to the Overworld. I had taken steps to secure concentrated food, medical supplies, and other necessities, to be strapped in knapsacks about our backs. . . .

But before these projects were complete, the tempest broke. The report of the overthrow of the Dictator of Zu, and the statement that he and I had been suspected of collusion, had taken dangerous fire in the public mind. Demagogues, too numerous to suppress, had risen to warn the people that I was "conspiring against their interests." These charges, added to complaints about my conclusion of an "inglorious peace," could not but have an effect upon a public so far advanced in thoughtlessness as the people of Wu.

Worst of all, my visitor from Zu unwittingly betrayed me. It would be impossible, I knew, for him to stay hidden forever; but I had hardly expected him to reveal himself just when he did. Not that I blame him; when he came out of the rooms where I had told him to remain, he had expected to find me alone. But, as it happened, I was just being interviewed by a reporter for the *Screamer*! Too late, I saw Clay, on whose face a stubbly red beard was beginning to sprout! The knowing gleam in the reporter's eyes flashed at me like a danger signal.

To threaten the journalist, to offer him a bribe, would only have been to make him more suspicious, and hence more of a peril; my only hope was that he would misinterpret what he had seen. But only a few hours later the *Screamer* appeared in a special edition, describing the "mysterious stranger" seen in the home of Luma the Illustrious—a stranger whose "foreign origin" was evident from his queer appearance. It was stated that his eyes were of an outlandish blue, and that his stubbly hair was faintly red—a color attributed only to one man in all history. Rumors were current, the paper went on to report, that the outcast Dictator of Zu had found shelter beneath Luma's roof, and that Luma was plotting with Ra the Righteous against his own people.

The storm burst over us with cataclysmic suddenness. I had been having one of my many little discussions with Clay, talking over old times and planning for the future, when I heard a great thumping at the door, and opened to admit one of the guards, who entered in such excitement that he forgot the customary formality of bowing till his palms scraped the floor. His face, normally white, had grown red with agitation; his hands fluttered; his salmon eyes were wide with bewilderment and alarm.

"Excellency!" he gasped. "Your Abysmal Excellency! Quick! The mob!"

"What mob?" I demanded.

"Come! Look!" he cried. "Great caverns, quick!" And he started away down the long greenish-yellow gallery.

Exchanging frightened glances, Clay and I followed in silence, until we had reached the farther end of the palace, where the guard lifted a slit of stone in one of the walls—a fragment barely an inch across, just enough to permit us a peep through the partition, while keeping us safe fron observation.

Instantly a confusion of cries came to our ears—cries fierce, shrill, bloodcurdling. "Down with Luma! Down with Luma! Down with him! Lynch him! Stab him! Massacre him! . . . Long live Thuno Flatum!"

Peering through the slit in the wall, I witnessed a sight that made my heart give a tremendous leap and my hair prickle. Back and forth, through the gallery outside, a savage throng was parading. Hundreds deep, they moved with a swarming fury. Some brandished sticks and poles, some held ropes coiled into nooses, some waved faggots ready for lighting. At the same time, there came a battering sound from one corner of the wall—a din as of a sledge hammer striking.

"Glorious abysses! They're pounding down the gates!" whispered the guard, as he hastily shoved the stone into place again. "We can't hold them back much longer!"

"Can't hold them back!" I agreed, knowing that no wild beast was more to be feared than that mad rabble. And then, swiftly turning to Clay, who stood watching with eyes half popping out of his head, "Come! There's no time to lose!"

We sprinted back through the gallery, then down a side-passage beneath the palace, where we paused long enough to secure provisions, and to disguise ourselves—Clay by donning again the garb in which he had escaped from Zu, and I by smearing my face with white powder, exchanging my royal clothes for a plain black robe, and covering my eyes with dark glasses.

Already, from the palace above, we could hear the mob screaming.

"They've broken in!" I muttered. "In a minute they'll be down here!"

He nodded; and while the howling from upstairs grew louder, we started down a dark and tortuous channel sloping deep underground.

Neither of us spoke as we hastened along, scarcely daring to turn on a flashlight to guide us. But we well knew our destination—the base of the ventilating flue, where we had concealed the climbing tackle.

In a straight line, this point was not far; but, in order to avoid detection, we had to circle miles out of our way, through obscure and little-used corridors. Hours passed before we had approached safety. And then, for a few minutes, we had to risk a greater peril. Separating us from the ventilation flue was a stretch of more frequented avenue.

Trusting to our disguise, we stepped boldly out of hiding.

As we emerged into the wider thoroughfare, we found the people crowding back and forth excitedly; but, fortunately, none seemed to notice us. The scoots rushed hither and thither as crazily as ever, several of them missing us by inches; while a newsgirl squeaked, "Latest *Screamer*! Buy the latest *Screamer*! Super-extra-extra-extra! Great revolution! Luma the Illustrious abdicates! Thuno Flatum restored to power! Super-extra-extra-extra!"

"Super-extra-extra! Buy the latest *Blare*!" I heard from another side. "War with Zu breaks out again! Thuno Flatum sends troops to the depths! Huge turnover! Subterrain attacks renewed! Buy the latest *Blare*! Super-extra-extra-extra!"

Even as this cry rang forth, we caught a glimpse of marching helmeted forms, hundreds upon hundreds, tramping with a prancing military motion along a side-gallery, beneath waving green and vermilion banners.

At the same time, a turn in the gallery gave us a glance into the mile-deep vastness of a prodigious chasm. Far beneath us, in the eerie depths, we saw multitudes of tiny forms, drawn up in military columns and regiments; while, from the walls of the abyss, great shafts of lightning—white and violet, orange and green—began to dart to the accompaniment of portentous thunders.

But all these sounds and sights were swept from our consciousness by something still more alarming. Straight toward us, from down the gallery, a swarm of Third Class citizens came flocking, thousands deep, wielding spears, ropes, and clubs.

"Down with Luma the Illustrious!" they shouted hoarsely. "Down with Luma! Grab the traitor! Tear him to bits! Turn him over!"

"Quick!" I whispered to Clay; and we slid across the avenue into a smaller gallery, which, a few yards farther on, gave access to the ventilating flue.

"Down with Luma! Down with him! To the deepest caverns with him! Turn him over! Turn him over!" I heard the mob repeating, with rising fury, as the ventilating lid slammed shut above our heads and the multitude, not observing us, went shouting on its way down the avenue.

The next moment Clay and I had seized the ropes and hooks and had begun the climb back to the Overworld.

There is no need to dwell upon our adventures when, lashed together like mountain climbers, we accomplished the ascent through the air-tubes. Several hours later, thanks to my expert knowledge of the ventilation system, we had reached the outlet, and, for the first time in years, stood beneath the open sky, blinking in the bright sunlight and exposing our skin to the luxury of the breeze. . . .

It was days later when we reached civilization; had we not found water by melting the snow from the sunless northern shelves of the peaks, while nourishing our bodies by concentrated food capsules from Wu, we would not be here today to tell the story. Even as it was, we had reached the last stages of exhaustion when we stumbled into a mining camp near the California border. The startled miners had the surprise of their lives when two strangers, still dressed in the pointed hats and black skirts of Wu, came tottering in among them; and it is not surprising that we were mistaken for madmen.

But now that we have been restored to our homes and friends, and are once more full of life and activity, I do not hesitate to make the facts public, so that the world may know of the great civilization inhabiting the chasms beneath the Nevada desert. It is the purpose of Clay and myself to lead an expedition back to Wu and Zu, so that we may fathom their miraculous scientific secrets, many of which we have been unable to penetrate. We hope to set forth at an early date, for we do not know how soon, in their renewed strife over Nullnull, the people of the Underworld may blow themselves out of existence, leaving no more than blackened labyrinths and crumbling galleries to prove that they have ever lived.